To everyone who ever wanted things to go bump in the night.

TENTACLE ENTANGLEMENT

SIGGY SHADE

To everyone who ever wanted things to bump and grind in the night.

Content Warnings

This book contains graphic sexual content and elements that may be triggering to readers. Please review the list of content warnings to make sure you're comfortable with reading this book before you continue:

- Abduction
- Tentacle bondage
- Primal play
- Spanking
- Tentacle deep throating
- Double vaginal penetration
- Nipple torture
- Genital whipping
- Urethral penetration
- Humiliation
- Anal intercourse
- Workplace sexual harassment
- Murder

Chapter One

I want to use my sucking rose toy tonight, but the weather is so frigid, that I might freeze off body parts.

A cold draft tightens my skin as I step out of the bathroom. Cringing, I hurry through my studio apartment. It's up in the attic, and the heating should have warmed it while I was in the shower. But what should I expect in the middle of winter?

Frost etches the windows, turning into icicles where they meet the pane. I blow out a foggy breath and scowl at a cloud of condensation lingering in the air. It wasn't that bad outside... Was it?

I pull the lapels of my bathrobe together, the only thing shielding me from the weather. There's no way I can take it off and freeze.

A gale blows loud enough to rattle the window frame. I clench my teeth. Another gust like this, and the wind will swoop in here and carry me to Oz.

"Mate." A voice drifts in the air.

Shivers skitter down my spine, and a bolt of terror has my gaze darting around the room.

1

Moonlight streams through the window, illuminating the watercolor I painted the week before. I'm hoping to sell it in the coffee shop downstairs, where I work. Maybe if I could make some extra cash from my art, I could start going out, meeting people, and not being so lonely.

The wind whistles, sounding like a voice, and I continue toward the sofa bed. "Great. Now, I'm hearing things."

I pull back the covers and scoot onto the mattress, avoiding the coil that usually digs into my spine. Another perk of being broke.

My phone buzzes. I reach beneath my pillow to find a message from Jessika, one of the other baristas, that says:

Alexis, don't forget to watch that meditation video!

I click the link she sent me earlier, and it navigates to YouTube. According to her, she used it to attract a rich boyfriend.

Its title says, Call forth your Perfect Soul Mate using Dimensional Waves... Whatever that means.

It probably won't work, but a girl's got to have hope.

Thunder rumbles, drowning out the video's musical introduction.

"Ignore the shitty weather." I squeeze my eyes shut and dismiss the lighting seeping through my eyelids. "Focus on the soothing sounds."

I have an early shift tomorrow and can't afford to oversleep.

"Welcome to the nighttime meditation," says a soothing voice. "This audio will bring forth the perfect companion for your soul. Take a deep breath, hold it for a count of six, and exhale."

The recording goes on like this for a few more minutes before I drift into a state of semi-awareness, where I can no longer hear the narrator's words. Even the thunderstorm sounds miles away, a distant rumble on the edges of my consciousness.

In my deep relaxation, I try to picture my perfect soulmate. He would be tall, of course. I'm five-eleven and love to wear heels, but I tower over most men. And my voluminous, brown curls often add an extra three to six inches to my height.

What else would I want in a soul mate?

He'd have to be tactile—the type of man who wraps his strong arms around my body and cradles me to sleep. I couldn't stand one who shies away from hugging.

I want a man who is kind, loving, and generous. Who values a woman's company and what she has to offer and never demands that I pay for half. For once, I want a man to spoil and pamper me and appreciate my art.

Oh, and one who doesn't listen to alpha male podcasts.

And he has to be strong. Being both tall and curvy, I struggle to find a man willing to pick me up, let alone one who wants me to sit on his lap.

My lips curl into a smile as I continue the list. He's got to be wicked in bed and live for oral. The type of man who does it because he's addicted to the taste of my pussy and loves making me cum. And of course, I want a huge cock.

I try to conjure up an image of my soul mate, but can't picture anyone. Maybe if he fulfilled my list of desires, things like appearances wouldn't matter.

The thunderstorm drifts away, as does the cold and the wind and the meditation. Warmth fills my heart and spreads across my chest. Whatever this feeling is, I want it to last forever.

* * *

Hours later, I wake with a start. Sweat beads on my brow soaks my bathrobe, making it feel like a straightjacket. My throat is dry and scratchy, and my tongue tastes of ashes.

"Shit." I pull off the covers.

I left the heating on the entire night and slept in my fluffy robe and socks. No wonder I'm overheating. I tear off my clothes and toss them on the floor, but I'm still too hot. When I get out of bed to walk to the radiator, it's stone cold, which makes absolutely no sense.

Maybe if I open the window—I shake my head. I'm not about to let in the cold. Not in the middle of winter.

The soulmate meditation continues to play, and I check the time on my phone. Its display says 1:45. I still have hours before my shift starts, so I flop back into bed and close my eyes.

As I drift back to sleep, a dark figure appears in my mind's eye.

"What?" I blink myself awake.

A man stands at the foot of my bed, his head nearly reaching the lampshade. Moonlight streams in from the window, illuminating his biceps and broad shoulders.

He's taller than a basketball player, but with the muscular build of a heavyweight boxer, and I have no idea if I'm hallucinating.

The air heats, making my room feel even hotter, smaller, and the muscles of my throat tighten until I can't breathe.

This has to be a nightmare. Inhumanly large men don't appear in women's bedrooms, just standing there like motionless statues. I squeeze my eyes shut, and inhale a deep breath.

"One," I say, my voice wavering. "Two. Three."

When I open my eyes again, the room is darker. It's as though a cloud has drifted over the moon and sucked out the light.

But the tall figure is still standing at the end of the bed.

With fingers that won't stop trembling, I pinch my thigh, hoping the pain might snap me out of the dream.

Nothing happens.

"Hello?" I whisper.

He drifts closer like a wraith. That's when tendrils of doubt creep out from the farthest corners of my mind. Maybe this isn't a vivid nightmare.

"Hello, my love," he says in a voice that's deep and dark and melded into the shadows. It's the same sonorous sound I heard earlier when I thought the wind had spoken.

"Who the hell are you?" I ask, my voice a dry rasp.

"Your soulmate."

"What?"

"Your soul called to mine from across the dimensions."

"No I didn't—" My teeth click shut because my brain finally catches up with what he's saying. "Listen, if you're talking about that soulmate meditation, it was a mistake, alright?"

He tilts his head in a silent request for more information.

"It was just a recording I got from the internet." I reach for my phone and show him the screen. "See? It says forty-thousand plays. Everyone's listening to it, not just me."

Silence stretches out for a few heartbeats and the room darkens further, consuming the man's shape. Just as I'm about to dismiss his presence as a lucid dream, he speaks.

"That is not why I am here."

I straighten. "Then why—"

"I heard your summons."

"No." I squeeze my eyes shut, breathe hard, and try to meditate myself out of this nightmare. Because this cannot be real.

"Forgive me," he says.

I stiffen. "For what?"

"You are unsettled."

A hysterical laugh bubbles up from my chest, and I snap

my eyes open to find him still standing close enough to reach down and grab my feet.

"Of course I am... How did you put it? Unsettled." I fling out an arm and point to the door. "Get out of my room before I call the police... Or an exorcist."

"As you wish."

At his words, some of the tightness in my chest loosens. Part of me expects him to hang around for a bit longer, maybe even do something nefarious, but as intruders go, this one is unusually polite.

But seconds later, he remains in place.

"What are you doing?" I fumble about for my phone, but my fingers brush against my clit-sucking rose toy. "Leave."

The intruder spreads his arms wide, stretching them across the room until they, too, meld with the shadows.

Wait a damn minute. This is no intruder.

He's a monster!

I toss a pillow at him, but a shadowy tentacle shoots out from his torso and catches it.

My stomach plummets into the mattress.

Tentacles, now?

"What is this?" he asks.

Not even attempting to answer, I swing my legs out of bed and dash across the room toward the door. I don't care that I'm naked, nor do I care that my tits are bouncing painfully and hard—I need every ounce of energy to concentrate on speed.

Mr. Roberts lives downstairs. If I can get into the hallway and call for help—

A cool, slippery appendage coils around my waist, making me gasp.

"Help—"

Another tentacle wraps around my mouth, creating a gag

I run on the spot, launch myself forward, and dig my fingers beneath the slimy thing to wrench myself free, but he holds onto me like I'm his property.

No matter how hard I writhe and wriggle, I still can't break free. The monster's tentacles slither over my thighs, my knees, and my ankles, until I can no longer move. They even bind my wrists behind my back.

He lifts me off my feet and reels me in like a caught fish.

Panic explodes across my chest and I hyperventilate. This is worse than any tentacle porn I've read online because it's real.

The monster wrenches my shoulders back, jutting my chest forward. Every ragged breath makes my nipples tingle, which is a strange thing to think about considering I'm about to die.

Tears fill my eyes and slide down my cheeks as I wait for the inevitable.

I haven't seen the monster's face, but in a minute, I'm sure he'll open up a gaping maw filled with teeth. But he doesn't.

Instead, he says in a voice that seems to come from every corner of the room, "Come, my mate. We must leave for my dimension."

Chapter Two

The monster's tentacles are everywhere—around my waist, between my thighs, and circling my breasts.

My entire body tingles as I writhe within his grip, and I'm sure some of his suckers are pulling at my flesh.

The pulse between my ears pounds so hard that it muffles all sound, including the meditation I'd stupidly played to attract a soul mate. Had I heard him right? He can't be taking me to his dimension. Dimensions are a thing of science fiction. They don't even exist.

But a few minutes ago, I would have said that monsters were figments of overactive imaginations. Now, I'm suspended three feet off the wooden floorboards by a creature of shadow and tentacles.

My gaze whips around the room. All I see is the dark. Either he disappeared the moment the clouds covered the moon or this monster really is made of shadows.

"Calm down," I tell myself around the tentacle gag.

"Who are you speaking to?" he asks.

I scream, but the sound is muffled.

Shit. I need to get my head together. Panicking like this

will only get me dragged to hell or wherever it is the monster lives.

Maybe if I could convince him he's making a mistake, he might leave me alone?

"Please," I say through the gag. This time, the tentacle around my mouth loosens to allow me to make a sound.

"Speak," he says in a voice of smoke.

"I have work tomorrow, and..." My voice trails off. Is that the best I can say under the circumstances?

"Where we're going, my mate will never need to toil."

The clouds concealing the moon part, flooding the room with silver light. I follow the tentacle to find his shadowy outline.

"Please, sir," I say, "I don't want to leave my apartment."

The monster raises his arm in a slicing motion that causes the sound of tearing. My breath catches as a rip forms in the air. Shit. I'd heard of the fabric of time, but this is ridiculous.

What lies beyond my room is a landscape of volcanoes and fire. I would call it hell but even demons might find it inhospitable.

Heat floods the room, explaining why I'd woken up feeling too hot. He must have brought it with him when he entered through the portal. The air becomes acrid with a suffocating scent of sulfur. My eyes itch, then they water, then it feels like tiny claws are scratching my throat. I blink over and over, coughing, choking, gasping for air.

"Stop," I rasp.

"Do not be afraid." The monster's words echo through my ears and make my bones vibrate.

Any other time, his deep voice would be melodious, even soothing, but not when I'm about to die.

"No!" I clamp down hard on the tentacle with my teeth, making him flinch.

The monster pauses. "What is wrong, my mate?"

"I'm going to die."

He pulls me away from the rift in the air and loosens the tentacle gag a little further. "Explain."

"I'm human," I say through panting breaths. "There's no way a person like me could breathe, let alone survive in an atmosphere that toxic."

The monster hesitates for several moments. I can't tell if he's considering my words or deciding whether or not to take a risk with my life, but when he closes the rip in the air, I collapse with relief.

"Thank you." I blink away the tears, letting them roll down my face.

"Your face is leaking." He places the tip of one tentacle on my face and gathers up the moisture.

"It's called crying, and the liquid is called tears." I cough away the last of the sulphuric air and try not to react as he retracts the tentacle with my tears. "That atmosphere irritated my eyes and I was so scared."

He reels me closer, so I hover a mere ten feet away from where he stands. With the moonlight shining on him so brightly, I can make out some of the details on his face. Maybe the light is playing tricks on me or maybe it's the moonlight, but I can't believe my eyes. Part of me had expected to see a blank visage without eyes or a mouth or a nose, but he has the same kind of features as any human.

Arched brows, high cheekbones, and a perfectly straight nose. His mouth is wide—not monstrously so, and his lips are sensual and full. I squint, looking for signs of hair but the light isn't the best. He's either bald or it's slicked back.

I shake my head. Why am I checking out a monster when I should be trying to escape?

"Are you still afraid?" he asks in that deep, sonorous voice.

"Yes," I whisper from behind my tentacle gag. "I'm still scared."

"I know exactly what you need," he says.

"What's that?" A shiver runs down my spine, but the sensation isn't entirely unpleasant. When the feeling settles between my legs, I squeeze my thighs together and frown. I cannot be getting aroused.

Instead of replying, he carries me across the room, pulls back the blankets, and lays me on the bed. I'm about to ask what he's doing, but then he pulls the covers over my body and gives me a gentle pat.

Is this his way of apologizing for interrupting my sleep and trying to abduct me?

He withdraws the tentacles, leaving me alone in the bed, and then he backs to the corner of the room.

My heart sinks a few inches from its resting place. I'm not exactly disappointed, and I really do want him to leave, but I'm still curious about why the monster visited me of all people.

The tentacles shorten until they disappear within his torso, leaving him just an extraordinarily tall man made of shadows.

This is for the best, I tell myself. I can go back to sleep and forget that I was ever the victim of a monster. And by the time I wake up, I could dismiss the debacle as a vivid dream.

"Thank you," I say.

"I haven't done anything yet," he replies with a chuckle as dark as his outline.

I bolt up, letting the sheets slide down my breasts. "But you said you knew what I needed."

"Yes," he replies and walks around the bed.

"What?"

"You need comfort, calm…" His voice trails off, leaving the rest of his sentence unsaid.

My breath catches. "And what else?"

"Cuddles and caresses." He stands on the other side of the bed and pulls back the covers.

My eyes widen as he lowers himself into the bed and makes the mattress dip.

"What the hell are you doing?" I screech.

"Shhhh…" A tentacle coils around my thigh and slithers toward my pussy.

I freeze, my jaw dropping. This is unexpected. It's been a while, and I'm reluctant to refuse pleasure. "Excuse me?"

"Relax, my mate," he says in a voice so deep and hypnotic that I feel it in every fiber of my being.

My muscles obey his command, and I find myself slumping against the headboard. another tentacle snakes around my ankles and pulls me down, so I lie flat on my back.

"Are you going to kill me?" I whisper.

"I'm going to fill you with something calming."

Panic spikes in my heart, pushing me into action. There's no way I can let a strange man, let alone a creature of unknown origin, put anything inside my body.

I'd read the horror stories, seen Alien and a whole host of other movies—I'd be damned if I got myself impregnated and then consumed from the inside out by his monstrous offspring.

I fumble around the bed for a weapon, and my fingers close around my sucking rose. It isn't much, but I toss it at the monster's head. A tentacle snaps out of him and snatches it from the air before the toy even lands.

Damn it.

Before he can retaliate, I swing my legs out of the bed, only for a tentacle to curl around my waist like a whip.

"Mmmmm," the monster hums. "What is that?"

I slip my fingers beneath the appendage to dislodge its grip, but it tightens. It looks like he wants an answer to his question.

"What's what?" I turn to the figure in my bed.

"This weapon of yours is coated in something delicious."

I freeze. And blink over and over to see through the dark. My pink toy hovers close to where the monster's mouth should be and my breath slows enough for me to hear the sounds of obscene slurping.

He's licking my toy.

Heat sears across my cheeks and my mind fills with a catalog of solitary encounters with the sucking rose. It's been months since I last had a man. The last time barely counted since he'd suffered the worst case of premature ejaculation and then tried to blame me for 'being so hot.' Before that one, the guy fumbled around so much that I ended up faking my orgasm just to make him stop.

Dating apps are okay, but most of the guys there are either players, time-wasters, or catfishers. And then there are scammers like the Tinder Swindler.

With all my spare time spent painting watercolors in the hope that one of them will sell, it's near impossible to meet decent men.

The monster laps at my toy as though he's licking ice cream. My breath quickens, each hum of appreciation feeling like a caress over my swollen clit. I had only used the toy this morning and forgot to clean it, but if he likes what he tastes, I know a place he can get plenty.

"You're really enjoying it?" I squeak.

"I've never tasted anything finer," he replies with a low moan that makes my nipples tighten. "Where can I find more?"

My breath quickens, and my eyelids flutter shut. This cannot be happening. Of course, it isn't. This is just a dream.

I clench my teeth, trying to stop myself from saying the words.

The pulse between my legs pounds harder than my ragged breaths. Could I really allow a monster to go down on me? As the tentacle squeezes me around the waist, I quickly come to an answer.

"I can give you more of that," I rasp, "But will you promise not to use any teeth?"

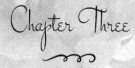

Chapter Three

I stretch out on the mattress, my gaze darting to the dark figure lying beside me on the bed. He leans close, his hot breath fanning across the sensitive skin of my neck.

Every nerve ending on that side of my body tingles in anticipation of those tentacles. I can already imagine what he'll do with them—the hours of endless pleasure he'll give every part of me that needed his touch.

But all he does is sniff my hair.

"Where's that delicious scent?" he asks, his voice shimmering across my skin.

"Pardon?" I rasp.

"The one on this?" He dangles the toy.

Heat rises to my cheeks. "You know..."

"Actually, I don't," he says. "And you never explained this object. Is it an implement for food preparation?"

I splutter. "What do lady monsters use when they're lonely and in need of pleasure?"

"We are creatures of shadow, and our females have mates," he replies. "Why is your face so hot?"

My throat tightens. It's not like I'm a prude, but I've

never exactly had to explain to anyone why I need to resort to sex toys. It's hard enough admitting to myself that I can't find a man I like enough to invite to my bed.

The monster wraps a damp tentacle around my waist and pulls me into his side. "You are uneasy. Have I caused you offense?"

"It's about the toy," I blurt.

"This?" he dangles the sucking rose in front of my face.

Moonlight streams in from the window, making it glisten with his saliva. I squeeze my thighs together and bite back a moan.

"Yes," I reply, my voice tight. "That's something I use for sex."

"Why?"

"Because I don't have a mate."

"You have me," he says in a deep voice that goes straight to my nipples.

"That's what I'm trying to explain," I squeak. "That thing you just licked clean…"

I gulp.

"Yes?"

"I use it for sex," I whisper.

The monster makes a disgruntled rumble and tosses the toy to the other end of the room. "You will cease the use of these items."

Annoyance tightens my skin. Monster from another dimension or not, he has no right to dictate my actions. "And why would I do that?"

"Because…."

Tentacles slither beneath my back, one of them wrapping around my wrist and raising my left arm above my head. Another does the same with the right, and two more snake around my ankles and hold them apart.

"From this moment, you will obtain sexual gratification from nobody but me. Is that understood?"

I jerk my head to the side, wanting to say yes, just so I can see how he could pleasure me with the tentacles, but I'm not ready to make any kind of commitment. Especially to a monster who dwells in a dimension that might as well be hell.

"That depends," I say.

"Explain."

"Let's see if you can do a better job than my toy."

His responding chuckle is so deep and wicked and sinister that the fine hairs on my back stand on end. I thought he would be a nice monster. The kind of simp I read about in romance books that the heroine would tame. But the creature pinning me to my bed seems to take my words as a personal challenge.

"I studied the anatomy of human women," he says, the tentacle around my waist splitting into four smaller tendrils. "Unlike the females of my species, you have many erogenous zones."

One of the tentacles wraps around my left breast, its tip flicking my nipple.

"Mmmmm." I arch my back.

"It would seem like my learnings were correct," he muses.

"What else did they tell you?" I ask.

"Shhh." He slips the second up my ribcage on the right side. Instead of the pointed tentacle tip I expect, the appendage splits into smaller tendrils as fine as string. Some of them stroke my skin, while others coil around my nipple, giving it a gentle squeeze.

"Fuck," I moan under my breath. "That feels incredible."

"I haven't even begun," the monster murmurs.

"W-what else are you going to do?" I ask, already imagining him doing the same to my clit.

"Where can I find that delicious substance from earlier?" He rubs slow circles around my left nipple, making me bite down on my bottom lip.

Arousal surges down between my legs, which aches and clenches for one of those tentacles. I arch my back and moan.

"It came from my pussy."

The monster pauses. "Where?"

"V-vagina," I say with a groan.

He rubs my belly with the other two tentacles as though preparing me for something ominous.

"What are you doing?" I ask.

"Making sure you have enough room."

My head snaps up. "For what?"

"Easy now," he says, sliding a tentacle around my shoulders. "I promise to make this experience pleasurable."

My limbs tremble with a full-body shudder. What on earth is he going to do next?

"Tell me?" I say.

"Human women are delicate according to what I learned," he murmurs. "You need ample preparation for a full mating."

My eyes widen. "But I haven't agreed to anything yet!"

"By the time I'm ready to mate you, you'll be begging for it," he replies, his voice soothing. "Now, lie back, relax, and let me prepare you."

I'm curious and partially convinced this is a vivid dream.

Why not?

"Fine." I let my knees flop to the sides. "But the moment I say stop—"

"Then I will cease giving you pleasure."

The pulse at my clit quickens. When he puts it like that...

"Go on, then."

The monster's tentacles massage up and down my inner thighs, their tips ghosting against the outer edges of my pussy before returning to my knees. Up and down he strokes, caressing my heated flesh until all sensation concentrates in my core.

My breath shallows and I buck my hips, trying to get him to at least graze my folds. But each time he gets even the nearest bit close to where I need his touch most, the tentacle skitters away.

I grind my teeth with frustration.

"Just touch me," I growl.

"Not yet."

His voice sounds on the outer shell of my ear, and the skin there tingles with his warm breath, sending ripples of sensation down my neck, across my scalp, and around to my other ear. Even his acoustics give me a surround sound of pleasure.

He's so close to me now that my breath catches. Moments ago, he was on the other side of the mattress. How did he do that?

I throw my head back, squeeze my eyes closed and focus on the sensations. By now, the monster has worked out that I prefer the flicking motion on my nipples instead of the tiny tendrils. But he splits the tip of his tentacle into two pliable digits that roll my sensitive flesh between his fingers.

Sweat beads across my skin. Not just from the heat, but from the intensity of the arousal.

"I never knew my nipples were so sensitive," I say with a moan.

"More proof that we're mates," he replies, sounding proud.

"What do you mean?"

"Our kind secretes a pheromone in the presence of our one true compatible female," he says as he squeezes both nipples.

The most pleasurable sensation explodes across both breasts and races down to my hungry core.

"Please," I cry.

"Please, what?" He hovers so close that his cool temperature radiates across one side of my body, but he doesn't touch me with anything except for the tentacles. "Tell me with your words."

I pant hard as those thick appendages tease my inner thigh, getting near to my pussy but missing it by millimeters.

"Why aren't you touching me?" I say with a loud gasp.

"Permission seems important to you," he replies, matter-of-factly. "And I won't move onto phase three until you give me your enthusiastic consent."

I'm about to scream at the monster to just stick it in me when his words register. If phase one is invading my room and making contact, and two involves climbing into bed with me and teasing my nipples, what on earth is next?

"What are these phases?" I ask.

"Nothing you won't enjoy," he rumbles. "Now, may I have your permission to move on to the next?"

"Only if it involves touching my pussy with your tentacles," I reply.

Without another word, the monster slides the tip of his appendage over the outer edges of my pussy lips, sending tingles up my spine. My back arches as he rubs up and down, each stroke moving tortuously slowly toward my core.

I've never had a man—monster or otherwise—touch me with such patience, such unending control. Most would rush straight to my opening, but not him.

"You are needy," he says, his voice lilting with amusement.

"I'm just not used to the slow pace," I say through clenched teeth. "And why is the other tentacle still stroking my thigh?"

"Because I'm waiting for permission."

"For what?"

"To stick it in your anus."

Chapter Four

I gape up into the shadows, my asshole clenching with shock. As the moon is hidden behind the shadows again, I can't see the outline of the monster, but I sure as hell can feel him. Especially when he inches toward me on the bed, making the mattress dip further.

On instinct, my hand clenches the bedposts, which is the only thing I can grab onto, since he's bound my wrists and ankles with those strong tentacles.

"Did I hear you right?" I whisper.

He pauses the delicious, pinching motion he was making on my nipples, putting an end to my pleasure. Even the tentacle tip on my pussy pauses, leaving me feeling left out in the cold.

"What did you hear?" The monster asks, sounding guarded.

"You want to stick your tentacle up my ass."

"Rectum."

"Same thing."

"I sense you are resistant to the idea," he says.

I splutter. "Because I've never—"

"Your rectum has its maidenhood intact?"

It takes a moment for me to realize he's asking whether my ass is a virgin. What a question, but then this is a creature who invaded my room from another dimension and planned to carry me off.

"Yes," I reply, my words crisp. "I am an anal virgin and would like to stay that way."

He doesn't say anything, letting the silence draw out until it becomes oppressive.

"What?" I snap.

"Where I come from, the females find that part of their bodies most arousing."

"Do they have tentacles, too?"

"No, but they have more holes."

I have no idea why, but hearing that makes me feel a little inadequate. Clearing my throat, I shake off my insecurities and turn to face the abyss of darkness taking up half the bed.

"No anal," I say. "Not until I give you permission, is that understood?"

"Of course, my mate," he replies a little too smoothly.

My eyes narrow into the dark. "I mean it."

"I heard you the first time." The tentacles on my nipples twitch. "May I resume preparations?"

"For what?"

"You're secreting that delicious substance. I wish to generate enough for a feast."

Bloody hell. He's planning to go down on me. As much as I miss oral sex, and as much as I enjoy the tentacle action, I really need to see his face, not just the glimpse I caught earlier in shadow.

Shit. What if he has spaghetti-like appendages for a mouth or an octopus beak or a maw of gnashing teeth? I wouldn't want those anywhere near my pussy.

"I don't mind you scooping it up with your tentacles and placing it in your mouth, but no oral sex until I know you better."

His deep laugh runs over my skin like static, making my nipples go taut. "Very well," he replies, still sounding amused. "And now I will give you all the pleasure you permit."

The tentacles around my nipples squeeze gently, sending the most pleasant sensation down to my clit.

I relax back into the mattress and let my knees flop back open. The monster brings one tentacle back to my pussy, making slow circles from my entrance to the base of my clit. I arch my back and moan. He's taking it nice and slow.

All thoughts of the next morning evaporate into the ether. He could pleasure me for the rest of the night and make me late for work. It will be worth it.

"This is the clitoris?" he gives it a gentle tap with the pointed end of his appendage.

"Ahhh, yes," I say.

"I noticed that the object you threw at me had a small hollow in the middle. Am I correct in assuming that it was a receptacle?"

The monster has a clinical way of talking, but I think I get the gist. "If you're asking if I put my clit in it, the answer is yes."

"And then what happened?" He rubs a tight circle around my clit.

"It sucked."

"Interesting."

"What?"

"I could do that for you if you want." He pauses and adds, "With my tentacle, not my mouth. I could fashion a small sucker with tiny cillia to stroke your clitoris."

"I don't understand."

"They would act like dozens of little fingers making soft strokes up and down your clitoris. And of course, I would adjust the pressure and speed for maximum secretions."

"Mmmmmm." I exhale a long breath. The monster just wants to make me wetter, but that isn't exactly a problem, is it? "Alright. Let's try it."

Another set of tentacles wrap around my knees, forcing them further apart, while another snakes around my waist and pins me to the bed.

I suck a deep breath through my teeth. "What are you doing?"

"Holding you in place," he replies. "This requires precision, and I want you to remain still."

"You think I'll thrash about?"

"I can almost guarantee it," he replies in a voice so deep and dark that the muscles of my pussy tighten.

All this talk of tentacles is getting me overheated. I want him to stick a nice, thick one into my pussy and fuck me with it until I become a sobbing mess. But I'm sure his endgame is sex, so why rush to it when he can give me hours of foreplay?

"Ready yourself," he says.

Anticipation skitters up my spine. "O-okay."

The tip of his tentacle touches the tip of my clit, then it flattens and then hollows into something shaped like a dimple and completely engulfs my bundle of nerves.

I gasp. This is far more intense than the rose because his sucker closes in around my clit, forming a tight seal. My breath quickens. How could I ever go back to my toy after this? But when tiny fingerlike appendages stroke up and down the length of my clit, an explosion of pleasure makes my legs go rigid, and I choke.

"Are you alright?" The monster asks, sounding urgent.

"Fuuuuck!"

He snatches the tentacle away.

"Put it back, put it back," I yell, my voice rising several octaves.

"You enjoyed it?"

"Yes," I rasp.

The tentacle returns, only this time a little more slippery, making the sensitive skin on my clit tingle. I throw my head back and pant hard as the miniature tentacles go to work on stroking my clit. Up and down, each one rubbing at different speeds. It's like nothing I've experienced before, especially with the other tentacles toying with my nipples.

"Your scent has changed," the monster rumbles. "Am I pleasing you?"

"Yes," I say with a satisfying shudder. "You're a very good monster."

His deep chuckle makes my skin tingle. "You are a very accommodating mate. May I have a taste?"

"Sc-scoop it up with a tentacle and put it in your mouth," I say, my hips bucking.

A heavier tentacle slides over my pelvis, holding me down, while another slithers up my leg and runs slow circles around my opening.

"Ah..." I say through panting breaths. "That feels so good."

"I am glad to be pleasing my mate." He pulls away the tentacle and fills my right ear with a sound of messy slurping that goes straight to my clit.

I bite down hard on my bottom lip, not bothering to conceal a moan because right now, my clit is so swollen it feels like a raw nerve. It's never felt this sensitive, but then I've never been so aroused.

Pleasure gathers behind the bundle of nerves, pushing down on my womb with a blissful weight. It spreads to my core, making it clench and ache with the need to be filled.

My breath turns shallow, and sweat beads on my forehead. I'm so close, with my entire pelvis feeling like it's on the verge of an overload.

The monster brings down two tentacles for another taste, only this time, they form delicate suckers that scoop away the moisture. A little voice in the back of my head whispers a warning that I'm being molested by an octopus man, but I kick it to the outer edges of my mind.

He isn't hurting me and has been respectful, courteous, and eager to please. What more do I want from a one-night stand?

But he just called me his mate.

I clench my teeth and switch my mind back to the sensations. The tentacle enclosure that holds my clit captive tightens a little, forming a gentle vacuum that sucks my clit, releases it, and then sucks again.

My thighs tremble, and sweat gathers under my armpits, beneath my chin, on the skin behind my knees.

Bloody hell, he's mimicking the sucking rose.

"Aaah!" I cry.

"More?" The monster's cool breath fans over the shell of my ear.

"Yes!"

The little finger-like projections turn hollow and begin sucking on my clit. One of them attaches itself to the very tip and pulls.

An orgasm blows through my core, spirals through my body and tears a scream from my lips. The muscles of my pussy clench harder than any fist, pumping pleasure across every nerve.

My legs spasm and shake, but the tentacles hold them in place. Throughout this intense climax, the monster continues scooping slickness from my pussy and gulping it with gusto. I can barely hear myself panting over his plea-sured moans.

He holds me like this for several heartbeats, prolonging my orgasm until it finally fades and my body falls limp.

Just as he wipes away the last of my secretions, he leans closer and murmurs, "That was delicious, but you've only just whetted my appetite. I need much, much more."

Chapter Five

The monster keeps me up for the rest of the night with his tentacles, making me climax over and over until my throat becomes hoarse from screaming, and I can barely breathe. As the first streams of sunlight filter through the window, he releases his hold on me and disappears into the shadows.

By then, I'm so exhausted that my eyelids flutter shut and I drift back off into the most peaceful sleep I've had in years. My body feels boneless, and my mind floats in the clouds. Before I know it, my phone buzzes and startles me awake.

Sunlight streams in through my windows and onto my face, making me flinch.

"What the hell?" I pick up the phone, finding the name Jessika Coffee Shop flashing on the screen. It isn't like her to call this early. It isn't like her to call me at all.

"Hello?" I croak.

"Lexi," she whisper-hisses. "Where are you?"

"Upstairs at home." I rub the sleep out of my eyes and yawn. "Is anything the matter?"

"You're three hours late for your shift. Mr. Roberts was ranting about you, and we all tried to cover, but..."

I gulp. "But what?"

"He says if you don't make it for the rush hour at lunchtime, then you can find yourself another job and another place to live."

"Shit," I drop the phone.

"Are you still there?"

"Y-yes," I blurt. "How long do I have left?"

"An hour."

"Thanks." I hang up, swing my legs out of bed and jog to the bathroom, cursing myself for slacking.

This isn't like me at all. I have my routine and I'm always in bed by nine with a book, asleep by ten and awake at six at the latest. What on earth just caused me to oversleep—

Memories hit me all at once. The thunderstorm, Jessika's fated mate meditation, the dark figure at the foot of my bed, and the tentacles. But they are hazy—almost like a dream. Because no matter how vivid it felt, my body just isn't capable of multiple orgasms... Is it?

I stand in front of the mirror, finding red marks on my wrists and around my waist. My nipples are redder than usual, as is the skin of my inner thighs. Arousal floods my core, and I suppress a moan. Maybe I got tangled up in the sheets and did it to myself? Stranger things have happened in books.

Raising a hand, I brush my fingertips over my nipple and shiver. They feel raw, as though someone has pulled and pinched them for hours.

"Shit" I mutter under my breath. The pheromone must have kept me from freaking out because I'd never get freaky with a tentacle monster.

"It was all real. But how?"

The sun disappears behind a cloud, casting the bathroom in shadow. I step into the bath, turn on the hot spray and cover myself in shower gel. Every inch of my skin feels tender from the monster's touch. His tentacles were everywhere last night, and what he did to my clit was beyond description.

If I had the time, and if my body wasn't feeling so raw, I would rub myself to orgasm. But for once in my entire existence, I feel strangely fulfilled.

"What would have happened if I'd let him penetrate me?" The muscles of my core pulse in protest. I ignore them and step out of the shower.

It's one thing to allow a creature of unknown origin to grope me under the covers. Quite another to let him get me pregnant.

I run down the stairs to find a long line curving around the coffee shop's interior. My watercolors hang on the walls, but I'm too agitated to notice if anyone is looking at the paintings.

Mr. Roberts stands beside the counter with his arms folded across his chest, glaring down at me like I'm a naughty schoolgirl. He's one of the few people who tower over me, even when I'm wearing shoes with a thick platform. This morning, he looks like he wants to eviscerate me with his glower.

"Alexis," he says, his words clipped. "Come with me."

My heart skips a beat. He usually enjoys yelling at people in public or firing them on the spot. If I have to speak to him in private then this has to be a huge deal.

Without another word, he turns on his heel, and I follow him around the counter and to the back. His office is at the far end of the employee changing room, a locker-lined space nobody uses because it's overlooked by Mr. Roberts's glass-fronted room.

Today, the blinds are closed, which means nobody can see if he's planning on throttling me. Shaking off the anxiety, I stare at his narrow shoulders. Mr. Roberts is all bark, but usually backs down when someone stands up to him and growls.

He holds the door open, waits for me to step inside, and then shuts it with a click.

"This is a delicate matter," he says.

My stomach plummets, and I try not to clap a hand over my mouth. He's going to fire me. Fire me and then tell me to clear my things from the attic.

Mr. Roberts folds his arms across his chest. "Can you explain the loud noises that came from your apartment last night?"

I step back, my jaw dropping. "Sorry, what?"

He winces. "What employees do in their own time is no business of the company."

"Okay..." I wait for him to get to the point.

"And as a valued member of our barista crew, it disappoints me to discover that you failed to turn up at your shift due to lewd behavior."

On the inside, I'm cringing. Last night had been so noisy, there was no doubt to anyone in the apartment below that I was getting fucked. But that's beside the point. He has no right to bring up my sex life.

I pull back my shoulder and look him dead in his beady eyes. If he was that concerned about my being late for work, he would knock on the door or even call. He's probably just annoyed that one of us is finally getting laid because all I hear from the downstairs apartment are the sounds of his computer games.

"I apologize for being late, talking about the reasons why is unprofessional."

His lips thin. "It isn't when your nighttime activities burden your teammates and disappoint our customers."

"You're being inappropriate," I say through clenched teeth. "But I won't be late again,"

His gaze sweeps down my uniform and settles on my wide hips. "See to it that it doesn't."

If I wasn't one paycheck away from being homeless, I would tell him where to stick his job. But I can't. Mr. Roberts provides me with employment, accommodation, and the attic space I need to complete my work. He even agreed to display my paintings for sale, even though nobody wants to pay more than a pittance.

Mr. Roberts glares down at me, his brows raised in expectation. If this is where he thinks I grovel, it isn't going to happen.

"Is that all?" I ask.

Mr. Roberts nods.

I turn on my heel and walk toward the door.

"Alexis?"

"Yes?" I say without glancing over my shoulder.

"I didn't hear your man walk up the stairs. Is he a customer?"

I shoot him my filthiest glare. "That's none of your business."

Before he can say anything else, I storm out of the room.

The lunchtime rush is more hectic than usual. More strangers than ever mingle with our regular customers to order pre-made sandwiches, bagels, and paninis. Maybe last night's thunderstorm had caused more than just me to over-sleep, and these people didn't get time this morning to make a packed lunch.

After serving the bulk of the customers, I pick up a mop

and bucket to straighten up the store. It's the least I can do after leaving everyone short-staffed.

As I'm cleaning Jessika sidles up to me and murmurs, "How did it go with Mr. Roberts?"

"Don't ask." I shake my head. "Were things really that bad this morning?"

"Not really, but Mr. Roberts ranted about you making noise all night. It sounds like you had an amazing time" She gives me a sly smile and then nudges me in the ribs.

Heat rises to my cheeks, and I dip my head. "I didn't get much sleep, that's all."

"Are you sure?"

"Yeah." I raise a shoulder and wring out the mop.

"Did you listen to the soulmate recording like I suggested?" she asks.

My fingers slip from the mop's handle, and I turn to meet her smiling eyes. "What do you know about it?"

"Shadows? Tentacles? A boatload of fun?" She asks with a broad grin.

My breath catches. I glance around the coffee shop, trying to make sure nobody's listening. Mr. Roberts stands at the cash register, his lips tightening. The way he flashes his eyes tells me that I'm one step away from getting fired.

"Talk later?" I ask.

The conversation I need to have with Jessika requires privacy, and lots of it. If my monster is the type to slink around the rooms of other women, I need to know now, in case he returns.

Chapter Six

As soon as Mr. Roberts closes the coffee shop and dismisses us, I drag Jessika out through the front door. The sun has already set with street lights illuminating the busy road. Its rush hour with two lanes of slow traffic that fill the air with exhaust fumes.

"Where are we going?" she asks.

"You and I need to talk," I say from between clenched teeth.

"But I really want to go home..." Her voice trails off.

My lips tighten into a thin line. I know exactly why she's rushing back to her apartment. Hell, I'd do the same if I had an attentive man with tentacles to drive me to pleasure beyond imagination. The question is, how many women did the monster visit at night?

"Listen." I duck down toward her ear, making sure none of the passersby can overhear us. "That meditation audio you sent me kind of worked."

Jessika grins. "What have you named him?"

My brows furrow. "What do you mean?"

"Come on." She gives me a gentle nudge in the ribs. "The morning after I did it, I attracted Neil. He's now a writer and just signed his first contract with a big publisher, but he's waiting for the money to come through."

"Wait, what?" I say.

She raises a shoulder. "That's the only reason I'm putting up with Mr. Roberts's bullshit."

One foot stumbles over the other, and I have to hold myself steady against a lamp post. I know I'm sleep-deprived but I could have sworn she mentioned tentacles. And a creature from another dimension couldn't get a publishing contract. Could they? I'm so confused.

"You attracted a human?" I ask, keeping my voice low.

Jessika gazes up at me, her brows pulling together. "Sorry, what?"

"Um..." I shake my head, trying to explain what happened the night before in a way that would make sense.

Ryan, one of the other baristas, jogs up to us, his cheeks flushed. "Hi guys, what did I miss?"

Jessika glances from Ryan to me, her face a mask of neutrality. I wrap my arms around my middle and grimace. It's bad enough telling one person I was pleasured all night by a tentacle monster who feasted on my pussy like it was a banquet. There's no way I can divulge that information to two.

"I was just telling Jess about a powerful dream I had."

Ryan waggles his brows. "Do tell."

"Would you believe I forgot it?" I say with a high-pitched giggle.

She places a hand on my arm. "Are you alright?"

"Yeah." I run a hand through my curls. "Just ignore me, alright?"

Without another word, I break into a jog, leaving Ryan

and Jessika at the corner, probably staring at my back and wondering if I've gone mad.

Mr. Roberts has locked the front door already, so I have to jog around the back of the building and enter through the security door. As I bound up the stairs, I come to a few conclusions:

One, the man Jessika attracted might not be a tentacle monster.

Two, there's no way the monster who tended to me all night long was also pleasuring Jessika.

Three, before I go any further with the monster, I need to see his face.

When I reach the attic, my entire apartment is dark. Not that it's particularly spacious or well-situated enough to get ample light from outside. The window isn't large or double glazed, and I doubt that the space I occupy would satisfy any kind of building regulation. At least not with walls that can't keep out the cold.

I turn on the light and walk across the studio room, making sure to alert Mr. Roberts of my presence.

"Fuck him," I mutter under my breath.

"Fuck who?" asks a deep voice that whispers over my skin like a soft breeze.

I whirl around, my gaze falling on the sofa bed I left unfolded. The monster isn't there, so I glance in the direction of the little dining table for two. When I don't find him there, I walk into the bathroom and pull back the shower curtain.

"Where are you?" I ask.

"Close by," he replies. "Turn off the light."

I'm about to walk to the switch on the wall, when his words register as a red flag. "Why won't you come out and let me see you?"

The monster hesitates. "I am a creature of the dark."

"Like a vampire?" I ask.

"I don't understand that word."

"Do you burn up in the sun?" I turn a slow circle, not knowing where he's hiding because his voice comes from every corner. "Or maybe turn into a pile of ash?"

He chuckles. "Of course, not."

"Then why won't you let me see your face?"

Silence stretches out for several seconds, and I grind my molars hard enough to strain my jaw. Nothing is right about this situation. While Jessika listened to the soulmate manifestation audio to attract a published author, I got a creature of mysterious origin who tried to drag me into a dimension that looked like Hell.

When his attempt to abduct me failed on the grounds that I would die, I let him make out with me in the dark. Worse—I let him feed from my pussy. What kind of a creature did that?

"You're an incubus," I say, my voice flat.

"No," he replies so quickly I'm surprised he even knows the word.

"Then, what are you?" I ask. "Where are you right now?"

Another pause.

"Under the bed."

"Right, then." I reach into my pocket, pull out my mobile and tap on the icon for the flashlight.

"What are you doing?" asks the monster, his voice panicked.

"I need to see you," I reply.

"Wait!"

"No." I advance toward the sofa.

"Don't do this," he says, his voice heavy with a warning.

"Explain to me why not." I crouch at the foot of the bed but point the flashlight toward the ceiling.

44

"Our kind changes when exposed to the light."

"Like gremlins?" I ask.

"I don't understand that reference," he replies. "Please, make the room dark at least for another night. You wouldn't like me if I emerged into the light."

Frustration heats my insides until they sizzle. Why am I even hesitating? I should just shine that light and deal with the consequences. My throat tightens. What if I anger the monster? He hasn't hurt me... yet.

"Just tell me a little more about yourself," I say.

"Anything," he replies. "But please turn off the light."

"Fine." I place the phone face-down on the bed but leave the flashlight on. After burying it a little in the comforter, I walk to the front door and flip the light switch.

The room plunges into darkness with only the barest trace of moonlight providing illumination.

I fold my arms across my chest and lean against the wall. "Alright then, show yourself."

"Step away from the light."

Resisting the urge to roll my eyes, I walk back to the bed. "Come out, then."

"I'm right behind you." Firm fingers knead my shoulders, making my muscles melt.

"Are you touching me with your hands?" I ask, my voice filled with wonder.

"Is that allowed?" he asks back with a touch of amusement.

"That depends on your answer," I murmur.

The monster runs damp fingertips up and down my neck, sending tingles across my skin. "I thought about you the entire day."

"What are you?" I ask.

"A man who has finally found his mate." He threads his fingers through my curls. "May I undress you?"

"Men don't have tentacles," I say.

"You seemed to enjoy them yesterday," he replies with a deep chuckle.

This monster is avoiding my questions, and I'm not standing for this subterfuge. I turn around, only for his hands to disappear and to find him standing at the far wall. Moonlight illuminates his outline, and I can't help but wonder why he's so skittish.

"Why did you disappear like that?" I ask.

"Where I come from, it is customary for a male to become compatible with his mate before revealing his true nature."

My eyes narrow. This just sounds like another excuse to avoid showing his face. "What do you want from me?"

"Pardon?"

"I can't survive in your dimension, so why are you still here?"

"Your essence changes me from a creature of the darkness to one that is tolerable in the light. The more contact the two of us have, the more compatible I will become to satisfy your needs, but we must acquaint ourselves in the dark."

This sounded like a pile of BS, and his wording was peculiar. Is he a creature tolerable in the light or a creature that tolerates the light?

He's probably hiding a mouthful of tentacles or something equally as unacceptable, and he just wants me so addicted to the way he pleasures my body that I overlook his hideous appearance.

The monster takes a step forward.

I raise my palm. "Stop right there."

He pauses. "You mistrust your mate?"

"You're the one who keeps claiming that we have a

connection," I say. "If we're mates, why haven't you asked for my name?"

"Because I already know it's Alexis," he says.

"You probably read it from snooping about the apartment while I was at work."

"Alexis, please be patient." He spreads his arms wide, so they stretch across the room, just as they did last night.

Except back then, I was terrified. Now, I know exactly what I'm dealing with: a creature from another dimension who enjoys feeding on a woman's pussy, and I'm probably the only one lonely and desperate enough to give it to him.

One of his tentacles snakes toward me. The movement is tentative, as though he isn't sure if I'll accept his advances.

I step backward until the backs of my thighs hit the sofa bed's mattress. Sitting on the edge, I fumble around for my phone. "It's not that I don't trust you."

"Then what?" His tentacle slithers around my wrist and gives it a playful squeeze.

The muscles of my core pulse in anticipation. I already know where this is going and my body won't be able to resist the promise of a night of unbridled pleasure.

"I don't want a relationship with a creature who can't survive outside the shadows." My fingers close around the handset.

"I can," says the monster. "But you'll have to be patient."

My eyes narrow. "What do you need?"

"Allow me to penetrate your body."

"Where?" I rasp.

"Every orifice imaginable," he says in a voice of smoke. "You must fully accept me before I show myself."

The tentacle winds up my arm. I run a hand over the appendage. It's cool and damp, much like how I would imagine if I plucked up the courage to touch a squid. As the tentacle slithers around my breast and splits into two tendrils to work at my nipple, my mind flashes with the image of a giant octopus.

That's also when he secretes a slippery liquid that makes my skin tingle. It's probably a mind control agent that will make me fall in love with absolutely anything.

Yeah, the prospect of getting addicted to his touch before seeing his face sounds suspicious as hell.

Fuck this. I'm not having crazy sex with an octopus man who refuses to reveal his true form.

"Mmmmm…" His deep voice reverberates across my flesh. "I can already smell your arousal."

With my free hand, I pick up the phone and point its flashlight in the direction of the monster.

What I see next makes my jaw drop.

A gorgeous blond man with bright blue eyes and a perfect body standing naked at the other end of the room.

And there isn't a single tentacle in sight.

What is he? A fallen angel? That would explain why he came from a place that looks like hell.

My heart pounds hard enough to make my eardrums vibrate. This is just like the myth of Cupid and Psyche, where the god of erotic love married a human woman but warned her never to look upon his face. After getting consumed with curiosity, she shone a lamp in his face and saw a man of spectacular beauty.

"I wish you hadn't done that," the monster says, his handsome features falling.

"Why not?" I rise to my feet and step forward on trembling legs, still shining the flashlight at this vision of perfection.

"I wasn't exaggerating when I said our personalities change when exposed to bright light."

My stomach drops. "What?" I stumble backward. "You didn't say anything about that."

The handsome face turns cold, and his lips curve into a grin as sharp as it is wicked. "Light erodes our compassion. Now, I have no reservations about taking what I want from my mate."

Chapter Seven

I back away from the monster, except he isn't a monster anymore but the most beautiful man I'd ever seen. Tall, muscular, and blond with the face of an angel but the smile of a devil.

My gaze travels down his body, taking in broad shoulders, prominent pecs, and a six-pack so tight that my breaths turn shallow. Resting on those abdominal muscles is a long, thick erection with a rosy tip.

Heat rushes between my thighs. I squeeze them together and swallow back a moan. Something is off about this situation, and I'm not just talking about the naked man advancing on me with sadistic glee.

"What exactly did you mean about light eroding your compassion?" I ask.

"I'm going to bend you over and fuck you until you're oozing fluids," he growls.

"But I thought you wanted to take it slow," I squeak.

"That was before all the goodness in me burned out in the light."

My stomach plummets to the wooden floorboards. What on earth have I done, and how can I fix things?

I place the phone face-down on the bed, trying to make the room dark again, so he can transform into the gentle and kind monster from the night before, but the light switch flips on its own, flooding the room in bright illumination.

The monster's skin glows, but the look on his face becomes even more manic.

My eyes widen. "How did you do that?"

"Tentacles," he says with a wink.

I gulp over and over, trying to make sense of what's happening. "Where are they?"

He spreads his arms wide—regular sized limbs for a 6'4" man with a perfectly athletic build.

"But I can't see any tentacles." I shake my head. What am I doing, standing there, waiting for him to pounce, when I need to run?

I turn on my heel, and sprint toward the door, only for a thick tentacle to wrap around my waist like a whip. "Ouch!"

His dark chuckle makes every hair on the back of my neck stand on end. "I was waiting for you to attempt an escape," he says, his voice low enough to make my skin tingle. "The hunt is never fun if the prey doesn't struggle."

"Hunt?" I whisper, my heart pounding hard enough to disturb the neighbors. "Prey? Are you going to eat me?"

He shakes me from side to side, like I'm some sort of toy. "Naughty little mate. Would you like me to eat you?" The way he asks that question, I'm a hundred percent certain he's not talking about food.

My breath quickens, and heat pools between my thighs. "That depends."

"Tell me something, Little mate," he says.

"W-what?"

"How would you like me to fuck you all night?"

52

My throat tightens, and my gaze travels down his athletic form and settles on his raging erection. Men as sexy as this never usually show interest in me. I'd be an idiot to say no.

He grins, seeming to enjoy the struggle on my features.

"Well?" he purrs.

"I would," I say.

His brows rise. "Then you only need to ask."

I bite down on my bottom lip. "Please... Tease me, fuck me, use me all night."

My mouth drops open. Did I really say that?

His wicked laugh makes my spine tingle. "You'll have to do something for me first."

"Anything."

He claps an invisible tentacle around my mouth.

"Suck it, like a good human," he growls.

My eyes widen. "Wait, what?"

"You asked me to use you," he growls. "Have you changed your mind already?"

"Of course not—"

Something sharp spanks me across the ass. Another tentacle?

I part my lips and let him slip the tentacle over my tongue. It's warm and smooth, with a coating of something briny that reminds me of the sea.

"Good little mate," he says.

My insides warm at his approval.

I swirl my tongue around the tentacle, looking for sensitive spots or at least a way to take control of the situation, but his eyes narrow.

"More?" he asks.

I nod through my mouthful.

"That's it," he says, his voice breathy as he shoves the

cock-shaped tentacle toward my throat. "I knew you could take it."

The appendage hits my gag reflex, and I breathe hard to stop myself from choking. Somehow, I want to prove to him that I can take him all.

His eyes glaze with lust, and his tongue darts out to lick his lips. Tears gather in the corners of my eyes as he pistons in and out of my mouth. When I blink, they slide down my cheeks, but a tentacle slithers up the side of my face to catch the tear.

The monster stands in front of me, his huge erection within grabbing distance. Why is he making me suck his tentacle when I could give him a blow job?

As he builds up a steady rhythm, I force breaths in and out of my throat, making the tentacle fellatio somewhat survivable. My eyes continued to stream, but none of the tears so much as reach my chin.

"Look at me," he growls. "I want to see you cry."

My gaze travels up his glorious body and into that grinning face. He no longer looks like an angel to me but the wickedest of demons.

"This is what you wanted," he growls. "The chance to look upon your mate while we fuck. Well, here I am."

I reach out with a trembling hand toward his erection, but he slaps it away.

"You will earn the right to touch my cock, little mate," he says.

A shiver skitters down my spine. He doesn't even sound like himself anymore.

"Take off your clothing," he says, his voice thick.

I reach up and fumble with the buttons of my shirt, but my fingers won't cooperate. Not with every ounce of sensation concentrating on the furnace between my legs.

"Hurry up."

"I'm trying," I mumble with a tentacle halfway down my throat.

"Gah!"

Invisible appendages slip beneath my clothes, over my fevered skin. They slither around my breasts, between my legs, but he makes sure not to touch my nipples or clit.

As I continue sucking him, he rubs the tentacles over my skin, secreting a slippery substance like liquid silk. The gleam in his eyes becomes even more manic, with his pupils expanding. Any other time, I would beg and scream for mercy but my mouth is otherwise occupied.

This has to be a pheromone. It is the only way to explain why I'm not frozen in terror. I want him—cruel or not, and I need him to touch me right now.

"Please," I say around my mouthful.

He smirks. "What did you say?"

"Aaah..." It's near impossible to form words with the appendage pistoning in and out of my mouth.

The monster takes pity on my soul because the tentacle shrinks a little to allow me to speak. "Touch my nipples and clit," I say, my voice breathy. "The way you did last night."

He makes a satisfied rumble that I feel deep in my core. "You've seen me in the light. Now, I want to see you."

Before I can ask him to give me a minute to change out of my work clothes, he yanks the invisible tentacles apart. My ears fill with the sound of torn fabric, and I yelp.

"That was my work uniform."

He raises me off the floor again, dangling me close to the ceiling. "You won't be needing clothes," he says with another of those wicked grins. "In fact, you won't be leaving this place until I've fed."

My breath catches, but then I remember what he did to me the night before and hope he wants the same tonight.

Invisible tentacles tighten around each limb, and he

pushes me against the ceiling so my back lies flush against its flat surface.

"Do you know your tears are as delicious as your pussy?" he asks.

I shake my head, my heart skipping several beats.

He slips the tentacle out of my mouth, finally allowing me to breathe.

"What else makes you cry, little mate?" he asks, his eyes blazing.

My mind races. I can think of a dozen terrible things, but I'm not about to surrender those ideas to a creature who lacks compassion. No, I need to unscrew that lightbulb, so he can return to the monster from before.

"I'm waiting." He flicks a tentacle at my pussy, sending a burst of pleasure that makes me jolt.

"Aaaah! Ummm... Sad movies?" I say.

"I don't understand that reference," he snaps. "Tell me something else."

"Maybe if you played with my nipples—"

"That doesn't make you cry," he hisses.

My stomach flip flops. It doesn't, but I hoped to distract him with something I knew he found delicious.

He rubs his chin. "Unless..."

"Unless what?" I whisper.

"Maybe I should play with your nipples..."

The monster spreads my legs as wide as they can go, until my inner thighs ache. My heart thrashes against my rib cage. What on earth is this inhuman creature planning?

A whipping sound slices through the air, and a thin lash hits my nipple with a sting. It's a peculiar mix of pleasure and pain that makes me flinch with surprise.

"Oh!" Tears spring to my eyes.

"Very nice." A gentle tentacle slides across my face and gathers up the moisture.

I now understand why he pinned me to the ceiling. It's the least cluttered part of my apartment, and the monster needs space to swing a whip.

"Did you like that, Little Mate?" he asks.

"No?" I lie.

One of his tentacles slides over my wet pussy. "Are you sure about that?"

"Alright," I say. "It was hot."

"More?" he purrs.

Shit. I really should say no, but I'm so curious about this. "Yes, please."

An invisible tentacle wraps around my clit with a gentle sucking motion, turning what should be a frightening experience into something hugely arousing.

The monster alternates between lashing each breast, with another tentacle running up and down my folds to gather my arousal. Throughout this, he continues that sadistic smile.

I'm breathing so hard and fast, it's an effort to produce words. "You weren't interested in my tears last night."

"When I'm in the dark, I have no appetite for pain," he says. "Only for your pleasure."

Sensation builds up around my clit, making my legs tremble. This is so humiliating—I don't want to climax while getting whipped. I force my mind to stay calm, trying to push back the orgasm, but my eyes dry up under the intense concentration.

"What's wrong?" he snaps. "You owe me a river of tears."

"Nothing," I say through clenched teeth.

He whips one nipple, then the other, but I've already built up a resistance to the pain.

"I wonder...." He tilts his head, his gaze traveling lower down my body. "Where else would you like to be whipped?"

My heart jumps to the back of my throat. "I don't know."

"I think you do." The tentacle sucking my clit pulls away.

"Wait," I cry. "What are you doing? I need that."

"I'm about to give you something better," he says with a sharp grin. "Do you want to try?"

Sweat breaks out across my palms and shivers run down my spine. Am I really going to allow this beautiful monster to whip me there? The muscles of my pussy squeeze and pulse, needing something, anything, to stimulate my needy clit.

"Do it."

He stares at me for several heartbeats. I can't tell if he's testing me or if he's really going to do it. When he turns his gaze away from mine and smirks, my heart sinks. After such a huge build-up Is he really going to leave me hanging?

A sharp pain slices through my clit, charging up every nerve ending in my pelvis like lightning. My hips jerk as though I'd been electrocuted.

"Fucking hell," I scream, my eyes watering.

Mr. Roberts downstairs bashes on the ceiling, but I'm too lost in the sensations to care.

"Very nice," the monster says, his voice breathy. "This is exactly what I need."

"Oh, shit," I whisper. "Shit, shit, shit."

"What's wrong, little mate?" he says, his voice taunting. "Can't you take it?"

My face tightens. This monster is not going to defeat me. I suck in a breath and try to sound confident. "I can. But the real question is, can you?"

The second time he whips me, it's with a much thinner tentacle that coils around my clit and makes me see stars. I howl at the sweet agony.

"Beautiful," he growls as I cry ugly tears.

By the third, my pussy clenches and spasms with the need to be filled, and by the fourth, I'm climaxing so violently that every nerve in my body feels like it's been struck by lightning.

The monster doesn't have to whip me a fifth time because I sob—mostly out of humiliation. I'm not only trapped with a sadist but enjoying his torture. How is this going to escalate?

"Your face is contorting." He wipes my eyes. One of his tentacles swats at my opening. "There is now moisture in your nostrils."

"Yes," I say through hiccuping breaths. "That's what happens when a person gets overloaded."

"Hmm.... I will remember to limit the strikes on your clitoris to three."

A hysterical laugh bubbles up in my chest. "If I knew monsters were afraid of a little snot, I would have done something about it earlier."

He makes an annoyed sound in the back of his throat. "Now I would like to test your other thresholds."

My breath hitches as a tentacle pushes against my pussy. My thighs tremble, and I bite down on my bottom lip, waiting for him to plunge it in me, the way he rammed the tentacle down my throat. But he pulls back with a mocking laugh.

No. Fucking. Way.

This beautiful bastard plans on teasing me the entire night.

I thrash within my invisible restraints, making the monster chuckle, his eyes dancing with delight.

"Do you want to end this torment, my little mate?"

I should scream yes, but I'm burning with curiosity. My

clit feels like a live wire and he's the only thing I need to soothe the burn.

"Never," I whisper.

"You are an endless source of amusement." He loosens his grip a little, allowing me to thrash harder.

"Glad someone's enjoying themselves." I clench my teeth. He thinks I'm providing him with entertainment, but I have other plans. I need my kind and gentle monster, and I need him now.

Lurching to the left, I move toward the source of the light. I'm sick of being toyed with by this beautiful demon. If I tell him to stop, he'll just find another way to make me beg for his tentacle or his cock.

It's time to exercise my safe word.

He throws his head back and laughs. "How you flounder."

Ignoring him, I edge closer, closer, closer to the light until it's within reach.

With my left hand, I punch the glass bulb, plunging us back into the dark.

Chapter Eight

I slump within the tentacles as the monster lowers me to the bed, but I can barely feel the mattress. Not when my entire body still trembles with the aftershocks of that intense orgasm.

What's wrong with me?

No sane woman should climax while crying, frightened out of her life, and having her pussy whipped with tentacles. Yet somehow, it had been electrifying.

More importantly, what's wrong with this creature? He's just like Jekyll and Hyde.

"Are you alright, my mate?" he asks, his voice grave.

"What was that?" I ask through panting breaths.

"An allergic reaction to the light," he replies. "I was afraid of revealing my darker nature."

"Did you enjoy doing that?"

The monster hesitates, which probably means that he did, but now that his compassion has returned, he isn't going to admit the other part of his personality is a perverted sadist.

"I regret not explaining this element of our physiology to you verbally," he finally replies.

"You should have told me yesterday!"

I roll off the side of the bed and fumble about in the dark for my phone. It's probably lying somewhere, face-down, ready to fill the room with the flashlight at the first sign of jostling. I want it off. Right now. No way do I want to meet the monster's terrible side again... At least not for a while.

My fingers brush against the handset, which is fortunately now off. Maybe the battery ran out. Maybe it's broken. I clutch it to my chest and glare through the dark at the tall figure standing on the other side of the room.

"Why did you withhold that information?" I ask.

"Would you have bonded with me if you knew about it?" he asks back.

"Of course not," I snap, although I'm not entirely sure.

The monster visibly deflates. "Is there anything I can do to make you feel better?"

I'm about to tell him to disappear back through a portal to his dimension, when I pause. Do I really want him to leave? That would mean the end of my pleasure.

"Can you give massages?" I ask.

"Of course," he replies, his voice more confident. "I have studied multiple ways to please a human woman."

I place my hands on my hips. "Like what?"

"Human females have almost as many nerve endings on the soles of their feet as they have between their legs," he says in a voice as dark as the night. "I could pleasure them."

A foot massage does sound nice. "What else?"

"My tentacles could soothe every orifice, and their ability to relax you is limitless."

My breath quickens. "Could you give me some of that pheromone?"

"Of course," he says. "I can produce as much as you like."

I squeeze my thighs together. "And afterward, will you wrap your tentacles around me in a cocoon?"

He takes a step forward. "Anything you desire."

The air thickens, or maybe it's just the tension in the room. Moonlight streams in through the window, illuminating the monster's head and broad shoulders. Fortunately, this kind of light doesn't seem to sour his personality.

A little voice in the back of my head asks what the hell I think I'm doing.

If I had any common sense, I'd call for the police, an exorcist, or even Ghostbusters. Nothing good can come of spending a night with a creature capable of turning into an angelic Marquis de Sade, but I really do need a little tender loving care after what he just did.

He hovers closer. "Do I have your permission to proceed?"

"Alright," I rasp.

He runs one of his tentacles along the sensitive skin of my neck, giving me a whole body shiver that makes my knees tremble. Before I can even sway on my feet, he wraps a tentacle around my waist, placing an even thicker one beneath my thighs for support, and carries me off my feet.

"What are you doing?" I ask.

"Laying you on the bed," he replies, his deep voice swirling over my skin. "I will soothe the aches I caused and help you relax."

"Fine." I sink back into the mattress and ready myself for his tentacles.

I thought he would go straight for my nipples and pussy, the way he did the night before, but one of the appendages wraps around my ankles and lifts my leg a foot off the bed. When he lays it down, it's on something soft and damp.

"What's that?"

"I rolled up one of my tentacles to form a cushion for you while I work."

"That's really nice," I murmur.

"I hoped that spending three nights consuming your essence would tame my darker side."

He winds his tentacle around my heel. As it slithers past my insole, it presses and squeezes every inch of the flesh there before applying pressure at the ball of my foot.

Until this moment, I didn't know my feet could be so sensitive. I enjoy massages whenever I can afford the luxury, but nothing ever felt as enjoyable as this. The slippery substance on his tentacles soaks into my skin, infusing my body with a deep sense of ease.

He lifts up the other foot and lavishes it with the same amount of attention, making every inch of me relax, even the tight muscles around my shoulders.

"Aaah," I say with a sigh.

He chuckles. "Feeling better already?"

"You're going to have to work a lot harder to make up for what you did," I murmur.

"Of course," he replies. "I intend to give my mate the utmost pleasure."

"Good."

Four thin tendrils sprout from the tentacles around my feet and slide between my toes. The surprise has me curling them and giggling.

The tentacles become more slippery, turning the tickling sensation into something a lot more arousing. The next time he moves them between my toes, it sends pleasure shooting up my legs and gathering in my pussy.

My breath hitches.

"Ticklish?" he asks in a tone that implies he knows exactly what he's doing.

"N-no," I whisper with a pleasant shudder. Right now, I'm feeling quite the opposite. "What were you saying about taming?"

"My kind is naturally hostile to others who are not our kin," he rumbles. "My darker side recognizes you as his mate, but doesn't care that the things he does would make you cry. He is a selfish, domineering creature who would only use you for his own pleasure."

"So, there are two of you?" I ask with a frown.

"In a way," he replies. "The version of me you see can exercise restraint."

"And you enjoyed whipping me?"

"I did not enjoy your distress."

My eyes narrow. It looks like he doesn't want to admit that he liked being wicked. But am I reaching when I think he also seems ashamed of his actions? Either way, it's obvious that the cruel and beautiful creature is also him.

"How can I make that side of you more considerate?" I ask.

The monster sighs. "The more time we spend together, the more that side will see you as a mate to be cherished, not used."

He quickens his strokes up and down my feet, with the tendrils stroking between my toes so wet that the sounds they make become obscene. As he deepens his caresses, he sends more and more pleasure to my core.

I'm so wet, and the pussy whipping has made my clit even more sensitive. Without meaning to, I part my knees and pant.

"Are you in need of me, my mate?" His voice sounds so close that his breath tickles behind my ear, even though he still stands at the foot of the bed.

"When you're in the dark, do you look the same?"

"Not quite," he says, keeping his voice measured. "My

kind are shapeshifters, with skin capable of changing for camouflage."

One of his tentacles slithers up my calf with a movement that makes my pussy pulse. All musings about his true form vanish with the need to be penetrated, stretched, pummeled.

"Get closer," I say, my voice becoming breathy. "And massage me everywhere."

"As my mate pleases."

The monster climbs onto the bed, making the mattress dip. Anticipation skitters down my spine. I slow my breathing, trying to temper my excitement, but it's no use. Memories of the night before still haunt my mind. I know first hand that this monster is capable of delivering intense and unrelenting pleasure.

"Open your legs wide," the monster says. "I'm going to massage your inner thighs."

"Alright," I whisper, trying not to pant.

Two more tentacles slither up the inside of my calves, spreading the same lubrication that makes everything feel wonderful. As they reach my knees, I buck my hips, wanting him to hurry.

"I'm so wet and ready for you."

He takes a deep, noisy sniff. "I smell the sweet scent of your arousal. It is intoxicating."

I swallow back a moan. This monster knows exactly what to say to get me going.

The tentacles make a gentle zig-zagging motion as they ascend my thighs, coating them with even more slick.

"Why are you secreting so much liquid?" I ask. "I'm already relaxed."

"To ease penetration."

"But my pussy's so wet." The moment I say those words, I realized exactly where he plans on sticking that tentacle. "Oh!"

"Would you consent to double tentacle intercourse?" he asks.

My asscheeks clench. He'd also wanted that last night.

"Maybe just circle my asshole for a little bit?" I say. "Don't stick the tentacle in until I ask."

His laugh reminds me of his darker side, and makes every fine hair on the back of my neck stand on end, screaming red alert.

"What's so funny?" I ask.

"After a few minutes of anal play, I will have you begging for my tentacle."

Chapter Nine

The monster turns me around, so I'm lying on my front, but with a thick tentacle resting beneath my hips and shoulders to keep them off the mattress.

"What are you doing?" My voice trembles. This is new.

"I need you even more relaxed for multiple penetration."

My heart flip-flops at the realization that he doesn't say double or triple or even quadruple. "Sorry, what?"

"Shhh," the monster says. "I won't do anything you don't want."

Tentacles wrap around my ankles, pushing my legs apart, and the one beneath my hips tilts up to expose my ass. A cool draft whistles in from the windows and brushes against my wet folds.

"Aaah, I've never felt so amazing. How are you doing this?"

"The fluid only enhances what's already there," the monster says with a deep rumble that vibrates across all his tentacles.

"Oh." My cheeks grow hot. "Could you play with my clit, please?"

"You never need to ask."

Thin tentacles make their slow ascent up my legs and settle at my pussy. They slide between my inner and outer lips and push them open, exposing me fully.

Another thicker appendage, about the size of a blunt cockhead, circles my opening.

My breath quickens. I'm so sensitive to his touch to the point that I can feel the texture of his tentacle's skin. It's mostly smooth but with tiny raised bumps that provide spine-tingling friction.

"Are you ready for more?" he asks, sounding like he's standing right by my side instead of at the foot of the bed. Just so I know exactly what he means, he taps my entrance with the tentacle.

"Please," I whisper.

The tentacle pushes inside, stretching me open. Pleasure spreads across my entire pelvis as the tiny bumps expand. It's like using a textured condom, but with the studs made of flesh instead of silicone.

"What are you doing?" The pitch of my voice rises.

"Do you remember what I did to your clitoris last night?" he asks while making flicking motions over the sensitive bundle of nerves.

I moaned. "How could I forget?"

"My tentacle's cilia will stroke your inner walls, providing you with a more thorough experience."

Even as he says the words, the tentacle pushes in and out of me but with those tiny bumps moving in different directions to stroke my insides. There's no way to describe the sensation except hundreds of soft fingers giving me a deep massage.

My hips and thighs tremble with the onslaught of sensation, and I murmur, "What else can you do?"

A second tentacle slithers between my ass cheeks and traces loose circles around the hole. It's flat and wet, like a tongue, and also textured, making my pussy clench around the tentacle.

The monster moans. "That feels so good."

"You get pleasure from this, too?" I wiggle my ass.

"Every inch of my mate is a source of ecstasy," he says, his voice deepening. "Squeeze harder."

"Okay," I say through panting breaths.

Pleasure comes at me from all angles, and as the monster places two tentacles over my nipples, my arms and legs tremble. This is more action than a woman can handle. It's like being pleasured by two men, who aren't demanding anything in return.

The monster continues pumping that tentacle in and out of me with a rhythm that matches my rapid breaths. I'm panting, trembling, sweating. It feels like I might implode, but there's no way I'm going to tell him to stop.

Another orgasm approaches, making the muscles tighten. By now, the tentacle at my asshole is making up and down moments and has developed long nodules to softly scrape against my pucker.

"You are so beautiful like this, my mate," the monster says.

"Can you see in the dark?" I ask, already feeling silly. Of course, he can—he's a creature of shadow.

"Yes," he rumbles. "And the view is delicious."

"I'm so close," I say with a moan.

"I feel the change in your heartbeat." The tentacle at my clit makes a filthy sucking noise, adding a spine-tingling pleasure.

"Oh!" My hips jerk.

"I want you to climax for me, my mate," the monster

says as he pounds his tentacle into my pussy. "Right now."

The words push me over the edge, and I splinter with an orgasm almost as intense as the one he gave me when he was wicked. Somewhere in the back of my mind, I wonder if my body craves this other side of the monster, but I shove it away and ride through the pleasure.

The last thing I want right now is my pussy whipped.

Every muscle in my pelvis spasms with waves upon waves of pleasure. My arms and legs collapse, but the tentacles beneath me provide ample support.

As my climax fades, and my breaths slow, the monster rubs soothing circles over my back with another slippery appendage.

"That was exactly what I needed," I say with a happy sigh. "Thank you."

"Don't thank me yet," he replies, his voice light. "That was only the beginning."

"But I've already come twice today and multiple times the night before," I say.

"All the more reason for me to continue."

The tentacle at my asshole changes shape, developing little suckers that pull at my pucker.

Any traces of sleepiness vanish at this new sensation, and I perk up. "What's this?"

"Do you like it?" he asks. "Your flesh there is very relaxed."

I still, my heart quickening. Maybe now is the time to try anal, while my body is loose and sated. "Could you make a thin tentacle for me? Maybe about the size of my finger?"

"Of course."

An appendage as thick as my thumb runs between my ass cheeks, making up and down movements. I'm still so sensitive and boneless from my orgasm and I've lost my inhibitions. I part my thighs even further.

"That feels so good," I say with a moan. "But I want more."

"You want me to put it in?" the monster asks with a deep drawl.

"Please," I whisper.

He continues making that back and forth motion over my asshole but doesn't slip it inside. When he combines the movement with the gentle sucking and stroking of my clit, both my ass and pussy feel empty and needy.

But after several moments of this teasing, every part of me quivers with impatience. I turn my head to find the monster still standing at the foot of the bed.

"Why haven't you fucked my ass?"

"I'm waiting for you to beg."

Ah yes, he mentioned that earlier.

Heat rises to my cheeks, and I gulp twice. It's hard enough to admit that I want anal. Even harder to admit it out loud and then to admit that I want it from a creature of unknown origin. It doesn't matter that the version of him I saw earlier was beautiful beyond belief. He's just a sexy asshole. It's this version of him who I want to fuck.

"What do you want me to say?" I ask in a small voice.

"I think you know." There's a weight to his words that tells me this is important.

I lick my lips and wiggle my ass from side to side, hoping to tempt him to fuck it. When he continues rubbing me, I say through clenched teeth, "Please, fuck my anus. Please, fuck me now."

"Please what?"

"I don't know your name?"

"What am I to you?"

The answer is on the tip of my tongue, but I stop myself from calling him a monster. Nothing about his personality is monstrous. He seems kind and maybe a little vulnerable that I won't accept him, but he's always been respectful and never overstepped my boundaries. He chose me out of millions of human women to be his.

"I'm your mate," I say.

He makes a pleased rumble that skitters across my skin and concentrates in my pussy.

It clenches, needing the tentacle.

"Please, my mate," I say in a much clearer voice. "I need you to fuck me in the ass with one of your tentacles while fucking my pussy with another. Please, I am begging for your huge tentacles."

"Very good," he says, sounding breathy. "It pleases me to know you're so eager for my touch."

"I am." I turn around and give him a desperate nod.

Without another word, he slides the slippery tentacle into my asshole, spreading the flesh as it tightens around him.

Every inch of my back passage tingles with his strange lubrication—even more than my pussy did.

"Why does that feel so much better than I expected?" I ask.

"We're relying on my lubrication, not yours." The tentacles around my clit sprout thicker tendrils that stroke the bundle of nerves with a deeper intensity.

My mouth opens in a silent scream.

The monster gets about six inches inside my ass before reaching a tiny bit of resistance. He pauses for a moment, letting me adjust, and then slowly pulls out.

"Why didn't you go any deeper?"

"Because then you might feel too full."

I raise my head. "What do you—"

A second tentacle enters my pussy, but it's a little thicker, filling me so deeply, I'm sure I feel him in my stomach. My eyes grow wide. "Oh!"

"Double penetration," the monster growls. "And you're taking it so well."

He shoves the larger tentacle up toward my cervix, making stars burst behind my eyes. Just as I'm recovering from that one, the second slithers back into my asshole. I rock back and forth, trying to increase the friction. This is great, but I need something extra.

"You told me there would be multiple penetration," I say through rasping breaths.

"Want more?" the monster asks.

"Please," I reply, my voice trembling. "Give it to me."

I expect him to thicken one or both of the tentacles or maybe infuse them with bigger bumps. Instead, a third tentacle slips into my pussy, opening me wider. The muscles of my sex ripple and clench around the two appendages, spreading my body with shockwaves.

Double vaginal penetration is nothing I'd ever imagined and more than I've ever taken in my lifetime, yet it somehow feels perfect.

He twists the two tentacles inside me like wrestling snakes. I feel their alternating textures along my walls, writhing within me even as I pulse. All the while, the tentacle in my asshole moves faster like it's trying to match my heartbeat.

"Aaaah." I throw my head back. "That feels amazing."

My words encourage the monster to go harder, deeper, faster, until the sensations build up again. This time, pleasure coils around my pussy, taking on the twisty form of the entwined tentacles. The sensations become so intense that I have to squeeze my eyes shut, and I'm breathing so hard through my mouth that my throat dries.

The sucker at my clit pulls and strokes. The tentacles on my nipples tease them mercilessly, with pinches and flicks and a rolling motion that makes my toes curl. When the one in my ass expands an extra half-inch, the pleasure explodes through my insides and forces out a lusty scream.

This next orgasm is just as intense as the one he gave me during the pussy whipping, except I feel it from my core to my belly and in the marrow of my bones. My nerves sing, and every muscle in my body trembles.

Pleasure like this should be illegal or at least controlled. Because right now, if the monster asks me to return to his dimension, I probably wouldn't say no.

I collapse on him and the mattress, a boneless, twitching heap. All traces of tension from the memory of his darker personality vanishes under the knowledge that there's something that my body enjoys just as much as it had enjoyed his cruelty.

The monster runs tentacles up and down my back with firm massaging strokes, but the calming action isn't necessary. Not when the powerful orgasm has turned me boneless.

It takes a few moments to catch my breath, and I murmur, "That was great."

"There's one more hole," the monster says.

"You want a blow job?"

"I mean this one."

The tip of a narrow tentacle taps at a patch of skin beneath my clit.

I'm too lost in pleasure to be shocked but still managed to say, "But you're too big!"

"I know you can handle it," the monster almost sounds like his wicked self, even though the room is still unlit.

"Will you make it feel good?" I ask.

"You know I will," he says in a dark voice.

I bite down on my bottom lip. Do I really want the monster to fuck me in the urethra?

Chapter Ten

Why am I even considering this? There's no way a tentacle of any size could fit into my urethra. Hell, I can barely find the tiny hole when I examine myself in the mirror, and the only way I know it exists is when I pass water.

He strokes up and down from the base of my clit to a spot less than an inch lower, and I shudder at the thought of him penetrating me there.

"You're frightened," the monster says.

"No one has ever entered me through that hole."

"So, you are a virgin, there?" he asks in a voice as smooth as velvet.

Heat rushes to my cheeks. "Not just my urethra."

The monster makes a pleased rumble. "I am honored to be your first in many different ways."

I huff a laugh. "You're also my first monster."

His tentacle pauses.

That's when I realize he probably wants me to call him Mate or at least something not so negative. "Sorry," I murmur. "But I never knew your name, and…"

I let my voice trail off, hoping he'll take pity on me and

maybe fill the silence. The tentacle stroking my pussy twitches.

"What do I call you?" I ask.

"Mate."

"But what are you, really?"

"Another creature looking for love," he replies. "Much like you are."

"But I'm a human woman, and you're a male..."

"I am a creature of tentacle and shadow. My language is visual."

"Okay." I make a mental note to ask his alternate self if I'm ever unfortunate to meet him again. He seems a little less sensitive about his nature than my monster. I mean creature. Mate.

The silence between us continues for a few more heartbeats until he finally asks, "Am I so monstrous?"

"Ummm..." I bite down on my bottom lip. "You have a nice personality and you seem caring and easy to talk to, but in our world, there aren't many creatures with tentacles. At least not any that can talk."

When he doesn't respond, I blurt, "I keep imagining you as a talking octopus."

"I see."

My heart plummets. I've said the wrong thing. "Why does it bother you so much?"

"Our kind are shaped as we are for survival," he says in a voice that fills the room. "It pains me to think that you might find any part of me revolting."

I gulp. "Never, and if I did, I'd scream for help. Besides, some humans might call you very beautiful."

"It only matters what you think," the monster says, sounding grave.

"That time the light was on, I'd never seen a man so handsome," I say, because that was the truth. "When

I saw you in the light, I wondered if you were an angel."

"Yet, you call me a monster."

"You drank my tears."

"But?"

"Well." I shift uncomfortably on the mattress. "Whipping a woman until she cries isn't very gentlemanly."

Moonlight shines into the apartment through the window, highlighting his solemn nod. "I will do what I can to hold back on my more base desires."

Something in my heart lightens. Perhaps it's the prospect of being able to enjoy my shadow mate both in the light and the dark. I feel special, knowing he would hold back his wickedness just for me.

"Thank you," I murmur. "But would you be able to be nice with the lights on?"

"The more time we spend together, the more my darker half will understand the need to be kind."

"Is it like taming you?" I ask with a smile.

"I suppose so."

"May I touch your body?" I ask.

He pauses for a second. "You would offer me pleasure?"

"It would only be fair, considering you've given me so much," I reply.

"My skin is cool and damp in the dark," he replies. "You might enjoy it better in the light."

My stomach tightens, and the pulse between my legs pounds. Even though my shadow mate has gone to great lengths to comfort me, I haven't made too much of an effort to put him at ease. There's no way to assure him that I won't reject him if I knew what he looks like in the dark because I won't know how I'll act until I see him.

Now, I understand why he remains at the foot of the bed when he pleasures me with his tentacles, and why he sometimes lies at my side without so much as reaching a hand across the bed.

"Maybe I can touch you later, then?" I ask.

"Would you like to try urethral intercourse?"

"Won't it hurt?"

His tentacle stroking my pussy narrows to about the width of a hair and then winds around my clit. "I can make it feel extremely good," he says in a slow drawl I feel in my nipples. "This is a way to stimulate the most pleasurable female ejaculation."

His offer makes sense now. "Are you hungry?"

"I could always eat." His tentacle snakes around my waist.

"Let's do it, then," I murmur. "But if I so much as flinch, I want you to stop."

"On a monster's honor," he says with a voice filled with heat.

He positions me flat on my back, and opens my legs with his tentacles.

Several thin tendrils brush over my pussy, some of them circling its opening, others stroking my clit. I lose count of how many of them are working on me, but it feels like every nerve in that part of my body has come to life.

My thighs tremble, and sweat breaks out across my brow. Part of it is the anticipation of something new, but most of it is just me wanting more pleasure. I part my lips and pant.

"Is it in, yet?"

He chortles. "I'm just priming the spot with fluid."

The moment he says those words, I feel a tiny stretch, followed by the most intense sensation. It isn't pain or a tickle but a new form of ecstasy that steals my breath.

A shiver runs down my back. "Oh."

"Is it alright?" he asks.

"Keep going," I reply through panting breaths.

The tentacle burrows a little deeper, moving from side to side like a tiny snake.

"Did you know the clitoris is much larger on the inside of the body than on the outside?" His voice fills the space between my ears. "The pleasure you feel is from stimulating a number of nerves that trigger orgasms."

My legs tremble as he wriggles the thin tentacle further.

"Oh, fuck," I say through clenched teeth. "What are you doing to me?"

His cool breath gusts across my heated skin. "You like it?"

"I need more," I say.

The tentacle inside me doesn't just expand—it presses down harder, seeming to stroke me from the inside. Sweat breaks out across my skin, and every limb on my body convulses.

"Your reactions are delicious," he murmurs.

Sensations overwhelm my nerves. Right now, my entire clit—all of it—not just the parts on the outside, swell. I can't speak, can barely breathe, and my eyes are rolling toward the back of my head.

"That's it, my mate," he says, his voice as breathy as mine. "You are so close to climaxing, so close to squirting into my waiting tentacle."

His dirty words push me to the edge of a dangerous precipice, and my legs are now spasming and trembling. The feel of his tentacle stroking these new parts of my clit is even more intense than the pussy whipping.

"That's my beautiful mate," he rumbles.

I fall off the ledge of sanity and into a powerful orgasm that tears through my clit and pussy. Throwing my head back, I open my mouth and scream.

My pussy muscles clench in time with my pulse, making

my body thrum. A feeling washes over me like a whole-body sneeze, that lights up my every pleasure center.

"Did I squirt?"

"Beautifully so," he says with a slurp.

"Oh," I say through panting breaths.

My eyelids droop, and my limbs become heavy with fatigue. I'm still not used to so many climaxes, and it's been a long day.

"Did I give you enough to eat?" I slur.

He wraps his tentacles around me to form a warm cocoon. "Sleep. I will hold onto you all night."

I'm so tired that it doesn't occur to me to ask where he'll go at sunrise.

At least not until I awaken to his grinning, angelic face.

Chapter Eleven

The sight of the monster's cruel and handsome face jolts me out of my slumber. Breath quickening, I shuffle to the other side of the mattress, but he wraps his invisible tentacles around me like a cocoon.

"Where do you think you're going, little mate?" he asks.

"I—" My voice cracks. "I thought you would have gone back to your dimension."

His gaze sweeps down my form because by now, he's already thrown off the covers, leaving me lying beside him, naked.

"Why would I ever leave when I have found you?"

A shudder runs down my spine and settles between my legs. Despite being scared of this version of him, there's a part of me that finds him difficult to resist. I'm weak in the face of such immense masculine beauty.

My tongue darts out to lick my dry lips, and his bright blue eyes dilate, tracking the movement.

"If you didn't leave, where did you go yesterday?" I ask.

"I was out feeding."

Dread rolls in my stomach. "Pardon?"

"The only way I can exist in this dimension as a creature of more than just shadows is to absorb human fear. It's not something I would have admitted to you in the dark."

"Why not?"

"Too much of the wrong type of fear causes a human to disintegrate," he replies with a casual shrug.

I was afraid he'd say something along those lines. "Is that why you made me cry yesterday?"

The corner of his lips lifts into a smile. "I would never feed on one so precious," he says. "At least not all at once."

When my mouth drops open, he smiles so broadly that all the fine hairs on my body rise with fresh terror.

I gulp. "Am I in danger?"

"Never with me, my sweet."

The way he says that term of endearment has frightening connotations, but it's reassuring that he doesn't think of me as a potential meal. At least not a complete one.

"Could you release the tentacles please? I need to go to work," I murmur.

"You don't need to go anywhere," he says with a smirk. "Not when you have me to satisfy your needs."

"Does your kind have money in this world?" I ask.

He huffs. "Who needs currency when one has might? If you need something, I will take it. In the meantime, you will mate with me in this body."

My gaze meanders down his perfectly sculpted chest and abs, then settles on his erection. It's long and thick, adorned with veins and a rosy pink tip. The muscles in my core pulse. Last night, he'd fucked me good and hard with tentacles, but I want the real thing.

"May I feel it?" I whisper.

"You never need to ask," he replies with a wolfish grin.

"You'll let me touch all of you?"

He nods, his eyes sharpening. He even loosens the tentacles so I can release my right arm. As soon as it's free, he coils around me again like a cozy contractor.

I have no idea why he isn't being cruel this morning. Perhaps because he wants to have sex? Anyway, I don't plan on reminding him of his less pleasant nature by asking dumb questions.

With a trembling hand, I reach across the bed and run my fingers over his shoulder. The flesh there is firmer and warmer than mine, just as I would expect from a man of his size and build.

"Is this appearance pleasing to my little mate?" he asks, his voice lilting with amusement.

"Very much," I whisper as my hands trail past his collar-bones and over his prominent pecs.

This is my first time with a guy as good looking as him and with such a beautiful body. The fact that he's a shadowy tentacle monster makes me feel less self-conscious. He's seen me at every angle and hasn't run, so I may as well enjoy him.

When I reach the contours of his six-pack, I have to bite back a moan. "Why didn't you let me touch you like this last night?"

"My body wasn't ready," he replies, his breath quickening. "It might have looked human, but it was still cold and damp."

"What made the difference?" I slide my fingers down his long shaft.

He squeezes his eyes shut and groans. "You fed me so well last night."

My cheeks heat at the memory of cumming so loudly and even squirting. I cup his balls and roll them between my fingers, making him hiss through his perfect teeth.

"Will you be able to hold this form at night?" I ask.

"Not yet."

"What would it take?" I wrap my fingers around his

shaft. He's so thick that they don't even meet around the other side.

"Ugh," he groans. "I would never ask it of you. There'd be no point."

As I pump up and down his warm erection, tiny beads of fluid leak from its skin, reminding me a little of how his tentacles provided their own lubrication. Heat gathers between my legs as I imagine how this huge cock would feel inside me.

But something he says finally sinks in. "What do you mean you'd never ask me?"

He bucks his hips in counterpoint to the pumping action I make up and down his thick shaft, seeming lost in the pleasure. Not including the time he'd forced his tentacle in my mouth, this is the first time I've really touched him.

"Mate?" I ask.

His eyes snap open. Instead of the usual bright blue of his beautiful form, they're deeper, darker, and larger than the average pupil. My breath catches, and part of me wants to slither away, but I force myself to remember this is a creature whose tentacles had given me unimaginable pleasure.

"Call me that again?" he says.

"Mate?" I ask with a smile.

He growls "Always call me mate. Never monster."

"Of course." I squeeze harder. "Can you answer my question?"

His features pinch with concentration. It's as if my hand job has stolen away his ability to multitask, which is odd, considering how many places he can pleasure my body at once.

"Aaah, yes," he says, still panting. "If I took too much from you, it would reduce you to a bag of skin. I've already spent too much time in this dimension and absorbed too

92

much humanity to live comfortably back where I come from."

My jaw drops. "You would sacrifice that much to be with me?"

He gives me the most peculiar stare. It's like I've said something wrong. "I've finally found my mate," he replies. "Where else would I be but at your side?"

My chest fills with warmth. All parts of him have accepted me—not just the kindly version of him that pleasures me in the dark. Tightening my grip, I stroke harder. The liquid oozing from his dick provides ample lubrication, but I wish it was my pussy around his shaft.

The bed creaks with the force of our movements, and the handjob continues. Most guys would have come by now.

"Am I doing it alright?" I ask.

"This is perfect," he says with a deep groan.

I made a gentle twisting motion around his thick cock head and revel in the way it made him shiver. "Do you ejaculate?"

"I've been cumming since you called me Mate," he says through clenched teeth. "This human cock is too small a vessel for all my cum."

"So you make lubrication?" I ask.

He nods.

"Do you know how human males ejaculate?"

He bucks his hips and snarls. "Tell me about the human males who have dared to touch my mate. I will kill them all."

"Later," I lie. This monster seems the type to round up my exes and consume their fear. "But let's focus on your pleasure first. Can you fuck me all day and night?"

"As much as is required to please my mate," he says, his eyes deep pools of black.

This is the longest hand job I've ever given, and my arm

begins to ache. Maybe his secretions are having an effect on me because the pain doesn't register as unpleasant. Sweat breaks out across my skin, and my heavy breaths mingle with his.

My clit is so sensitive and swollen. It throbs in sync with my pulse. I buck my hips only for it to brush against something invisible and moist.

"Oh, fuck," I murmur.

The more I stroke him, the more lubricant he produces. His liquid is getting everywhere, with tiny droplets spattering over my skin. Wet slopping sounds fill the air with each movement of my hand, and my fingers now feel almost as sensitive as my clit.

Pleasure travels up my arm, down my spine, and between my legs. It's the most bizarre sensation, and I can't help rocking my hips against his invisible tentacle.

"Keep stroking," he growls. "You're nearly there."

So am I. My pleasure builds and builds until the nerves around my clit dance like sparks and all the muscles of my thighs clench. I still don't understand how he could make me cum with such little friction.

"That's it, my mate," he says. "You're doing so well."

"Aaah," I cry out. "I have no idea what's happening."

Pressure gathers low in my belly, pressing down hard on my clit. Except this time, it's more sensitive than ever.

"What have you done to me?" I whisper through a sigh.

"You're awakening," he says with a growl. "I want you to orgasm, now."

My climax crashes over me like a tidal wave, throwing my consciousness aside. All that's left of me are waves and waves of ecstasy that wash through my senses. The sensations travel from the beds of my toenails to the follicles in my scalp. I twitch with every pleasurable spasm, throw back my head and scream.

Warm jets of fluid spatter on my belly and breasts, coating me in a fluid that reminds me of the sea. I'm so distracted by my climax that it barely registers that it's soaking into my skin.

It takes a minute to catch my breath. "What was..." I shake my head, my eyelids fluttering. "How?"

"It's only the beginning." The tentacles cocooning my body loosen, only to wrap around my wrists and ankles and pin me spread-eagled across the bed.

It's like being manacled, only he hovers over me with a devilish grin and eyes that promised mayhem.

"Shit," I say with a tired groan. "I should have known your nice mood wouldn't last."

His wicked laugh makes my hair stand on end. "Now, I'm going to fuck you with my real cock."

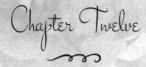

Chapter Twelve

I'm so wet, so ready, so needy that I don't care if he wants to give it to me good and hard. I just need to be filled.

"Wait a minute," I stutter. "Which cock?"

Amusement glints in his eyes, tinged with malice. Even though he's terrifying, a large part of me knows I'll be safe, if not a little sore.

"Now, it's time to make you scream," he says, his voice heavy with lust.

A knock sounds on the door, making us both stiffen.

"There's another male." His tone is sharp with accusation.

"How do you know?"

He curls his lip. "The scent."

"I don't know who it is," I whisper, even though it's probably Mr. Roberts. "But keep going. He'll soon leave."

"Alexis." Mr. Roberts knocks again, this time harder.

"He would dare utter your name?" my mate says, his eyes back to bright blue, all traces of arousal gone.

"It's just my boss." Reaching up, I place a hand on his shoulder and stroke up and down his bicep.

"What does that mean?"

"He's the man who owns the whole building as well as the place where I work."

"Tell him to find his own mate."

Mr. Roberts pounds on the door. "Don't pretend you're out, when I know you've got a man in there. I heard you the entire night."

My mate lowers himself to the mattress and releases his tentacles, leaving me squirming with a protest. As he rolls off the bed and stalks across the room toward the door, realization hits me with a new wave of terror.

"Where are you going?" I scramble off the bed and hurry after my mate.

"To kill him, of course."

A second later, the door rattles. I could only guess my mate is trying to open it with one of his invisible tentacles.

"Stop that." I grab his arm.

He whirls around and fixes me with a look that makes my spine stiffen. "Why are you defending him?"

"You can't go around killing someone because you find them annoying."

"Why not?"

Mr. Roberts bangs on the door with both fists. "If I don't see you at work in the next ten minutes, you're fired. That means no job, no apartment. Got it?"

My stomach plummets. He's mean spirited enough to make me jobless and homeless. Out loud, I say, "Y-yes, Mr. Roberts."

"He threatened you," my mate growls.

"Please," I whisper. "Don't do anything or I won't have a home."

His features tighten with a look that suggests I've sided with Mr. Roberts instead of him. I exhale a weary sigh. This is tiring—not just the all-night sex, and the pressure of having a job that takes me away from my art, but now I have a whole other person to support.

"Listen, I have to go." I head toward the bathroom.

"You will stay." One of his tentacles wraps around my waist, squeezing so tightly that I gasp.

"Mr. Roberts was serious, you know." I sweep my arm across the studio apartment. "You like having a bed to fuck me on? Or a ceiling? If you don't let me go to work, we'll both be sleeping in the park."

He parts his lips, either to demand an explanation or to say he doesn't care, but this is one subject where I won't budge.

"The park is an outdoor space where we'll have no privacy. If you hate the thought of my boss knocking on the door, you'll despise sleeping out in the open where all manner of men can watch us."

Several seconds pass, and my mate stares down at me like he's the angel of death, deliberating on my fate. I pull back my shoulders and hold his gaze. No amount of wicked grins and slippery tentacles could distract me from the prospect of being homeless.

"Very well," he says with a sniff. "But I will accompany you."

My shoulders sag. There's no time for anything but a quick wash, and I don't intend to waste precious minutes convincing him to stay in the apartment.

I walk to the closet to find a fresh uniform. "Either keep to the shadows in your alternate form or put on some clothes."

Less than ten minutes later, I enter the store through the back staircase, hoping to avoid Mr. Roberts. It's still early, but the coffee shop is in the thick of the morning rush hour.

The line for drinks not only curls around the store's interior but extends outside.

Jessika stands beside Ryan, fulfilling orders at one of the coffee machines. "Oh, thank goodness you're here," she blurts. "Two other members of staff called in sick."

I hurry to her side and start making drinks, part of me finally understanding why the line was so long. Mr. Roberts cares more about collecting orders than fulfilling them, which is why there are always more staff members at the cash registers than at the back.

'Who's ill?" I ask.

"Yvette and Maria," she replies with a smirk.

"What?" My brows pulled together. "Do you know something?"

"Alexis," Mr. Roberts barks from the back room. "As soon as the morning rush is over and you've mopped the floors, emptied the bins, and cleared the tables, I want you in my office."

I shoot the back door my filthiest glare. Sure, he's frustrated about being understaffed, and it was my fault for being late, but that doesn't mean he has to take out all his anger on me.

"Do you think I should point him to the YouTube video?" she asks with a giggle.

My jaw drops, as does the cappuccino I just made. Hot coffee splashes on my pants and spreads across the floor. "Shit."

"Whoops," she says with a grimace. "Sorry about that."

I rush around the counter to the back room and open the cleaning cupboard to get a mop and bucket. What on earth did Jessika just imply? The others had called in sick because they'd listened to the same video she'd recommended to me? The same video that had summoned my soul mate from another dimension?

Impossible.

Or was it?

There's no point in speculating. Not when customers are waiting for their morning brew. I hurry back behind the counter, mop up the spilled cappuccino, and focus on my work.

The next time I corner Jessika, I will listen to everything she has to share about this soul mate meditation. If Ryan's there, she can tell him, too.

It takes over forty-five minutes for the line to reach a manageable level of activity. Now, it's just the regulars taking their seats around the tables.

Jessika gives me a pat on the shoulder. "I heard what Mr. Roberts said. If you want me to clean up while you work the machines, Ryan and I don't mind."

"It's alright," I reply with a tiny smile. "He's probably watching all this from his cameras. The last thing I want him to see is me letting you take my punishment."

"Suit yourself."

"But we'll talk later?" I ask with a bit of bite.

Jessika gives me a slow nod with a nervous glance that tells me she knows the topic of our future conversation.

I returned to the cupboard for the mop and bucket, as well as a few cleaning cloths for the tables. On my way back, I notice a blank patch on the walls, looking like someone has purchased one of my paintings.

My heart skips a beat. Perhaps that was what Mr. Roberts had wanted to discuss? I'm about to return to the shop floor when I spot a figure standing by the door.

He's tall and blond and angelic and fully clothed... Mostly.

Do gray sweatpants count? Whoever he stole them from is smaller, so the jersey fabric stretches obscenely over his long, thick cock.

I stand in the doorway, mesmerized by the sight until one of the female regulars sashays over to him and tries to make conversation.

She's a cool blonde who wears red lipstick and form-fitting suits. When she tilts her head and bats her lashes, my mate acts like I'm the only person in the room.

His broad chest rises and falls with deep breaths. Is he angry? I glance to my left and right for signs of a man or anything else that would have annoyed him, but all the males in the coffee shop are either busy doing their work or enjoying their breakfast.

The regular who had tried to chat with him gives up and slopes back to her seat. Warm satisfaction fills my chest, and I walk past the counter and over to my mate. That woman has always been so snooty and never says thank you. It's petty, but I want her to see him respond to me.

His brows rise. "This is your work?"

"Hello," I whisper. "What are you doing here? I thought you would keep to the shadows."

"I thought you made art," he says.

"What makes you think that?"

He looks me dead in the eye, as though the answer is obvious. "I absorbed your tears."

"Oh."

That was unexpected. Taking his hand, I lead him to the only empty table, which happens to be next to that woman.

"Sit down, and I'll get you something to drink." Then I lean into him and ask, "Do you eat and drink human food?"

"No." His gaze hardens and he focuses on a point over my shoulder.

"What's wrong?" I glance toward the counter to find Mr. Roberts standing at the doorway leading to the back rooms.

He beckons me over, looking like he wants to fire me on the spot.

Shit.

Things aren't looking good.

Chapter Thirteen

I cast my mate a backward glance, but he rises off his seat, looking like he wants to follow. I shake my head, but he continues walking toward me.

"Alexis?" Mr. Roberts snaps, sounding impatient.

"Coming."

I turn on my heel and follow him through the back-room, through the locker room, and into his office, where he holds open the door.

Strong aftershave fills my nostrils as I edge through the doorway, trying to avoid touching him as I pass. Is he getting ready for a date?

"Take a seat." He lets the door fall shut with a soft click. Instead of walking around his desk, he sits on it with his legs spread.

I pull back the chair, lower myself into it, and try not to cringe at the way the fabric pulls across his crotch. "You wanted to speak with me, sir?"

"How's the painting going?" he asks.

I lean back in my seat and frown. "Um... Alright. Why?"

"One of our regulars inquired about purchasing several of your works, but she would like a quantity discount."

"What kind?" I ask, my brows pulling together.

"Fifty percent."

I bite down on my bottom lip. "That's hardly going to cover my expenses. Watercolor paper is getting expensive, then there's the cost of the studio—"

"Which I rent to you at a steep discount," he says.

My lips tighten. The studio is just the attic space next door to my apartment that's too drafty for anything but storage. Instead of voicing this, I say, "And I'm grateful for that and for the apartment."

Mr. Roberts narrows his eyes. "You used to paint into the small hours, but for the last two nights, you've been otherwise occupied."

I'm about to ask how he knows this, but then I remember he lives downstairs. The building is old, with wooden floors that creak with every step, and my mate and I haven't exactly been quiet.

"Perhaps if you took your career as a painter more seriously, you could improve your output."

Something in the tone of his voice is off. Or perhaps it's what he doesn't say. In his position, I would complain that my employee had been too noisy or that I'd been late two days in a row, but he's unusually preoccupied with my art.

Besides, it's peculiar that he wants me to sell it at a discount when it's already so cheap.

"You do realize that fifty percent of the retail prices means half as much commission for you?" I ask.

He leans back in his seat. "But imagine the exposure."

Now, it's my turn to narrow my eyes. "Why are you so concerned about increasing my output? It doesn't make sense."

Face flushing, he waves away my question. "Never mind

that. What were you doing for two nights in a row, making loud sexual noises?"

Normally, a confrontation like that would make my cheeks heat, but I'm so suspicious of this guy's motives that it barely registers that he's overheard me at my most intimate.

Mr. Roberts slides off his desk and tries to tower over me, but I rise off my seat and step back. He's six four but with a wiry frame that makes him look fragile.

"Answer me," he says, standing within grabbing distance.

"None of your business, and stop trying to change the subject." I ball my hands into fists.

He places both hands on my shoulders and digs his fingers into my flesh. "Without me, you'd be homeless."

"Ouch get off—"

The lightbulb shatters, plunging the windowless room into near darkness. A small stream of light seeps through the blind covering the door, illuminating my mate's shadowy outline.

"What is the meaning of this?" Mr. Roberts says before his body flies across the office. He lands against the wall with a painful thud.

I whirl around, looking for my mate, but he's disappeared.

"What are you doing?" I ask.

"He touched what was mine," my mate replies, his voice colder than ice cubes.

I breathe hard and place a hand over my chest. In my entire twenty-five years, no one has ever stood up for me. The backs of my eyes become hot. My mate just risked getting caught to make sure I was safe.

"Thanks," I whisper, my voice thick with gratitude.

When Mr. Roberts groans, some of the tightness in my chest releases, and I exhale a long breath.

"That was the man who knocked on the door upstairs?" my mate asks.

"Yes." I walk around the desk to where Mr. Roberts sits slumped against the wall.

"What just happened?" the older man asks, sounding dazed.

My jaw tightens. The old me might be concerned about my boss or even worried about being fired, but this entire encounter has been suspicious since the moment he asked about my output.

I grab the collar of his shirt. "You're going to tell me why you're so eager for me to produce more paintings when they don't even sell."

"What are you talking about?" He tries to rise, but a shadowy tentacle whips past my line of sight and wraps around his neck.

Mr. Roberts chokes. "Stop this."

"Tell the truth and I'll ask him to loosen the noose," I say.

"But it's some kind of tentacle," my boss grits out through clenched teeth. "Let go or I'll call animal control or the police."

My jaw tightens. He's exactly the kind of person who would get my mate locked up and subject to painful experiments. Ignoring his threat, I focus on the subject he's trying to avoid.

"What are you planning on doing with the paintings?" I ask with more bite.

"Sell them," he rasps.

"I gathered that, but to who?"

"Geraldine McCue," he replies. "The blonde regular in the business suit. She wants to buy them."

"Why?"

"Because you're talented."

"He's concealing something," says my mate.

I follow the tentacle to the most shadowy corner of the room. "How can you tell?"

"His scent just changed."

For the next ten minutes, my mate shakes Mr. Roberts until he makes a stuttering confession. He's been passing on my paintings to the regular but not the ones displayed on the wall. When I'm on my shift, he takes them from my studio and frames them, then Ms McCue sells my artwork in her gallery and keeps a fifty percent commission.

By the time he finishes talking, I'm swaying on my feet, and my gut churns with enough nausea to make me want to spit. It's bad enough that he's been stealing my art but having it auctioned at a fancy gallery?

"How much did the last one sell for?" I ask.

"E-eleven grand, but I can give you half."

My jaw drops. With that kind of money, I could afford a better apartment. Hell, I could afford a better life. "How many of them have you sold?"

"Once a month, I take a picture from your stack of finished art," he says through clenched teeth. "I've done it since you started here."

I turn to where my mate stands at the edge of the shadows. "Knock him out."

"Certainly."

"Wait—" Mr. Roberts rises seven feet off the floor, and my mate flings him against the wall.

When he falls to the floor with a satisfying thud, I deliver a hard kick to his side. Mr. Roberts doesn't even grunt.

"By the way, why did you turn off the light?" I ask.

"This is my most powerful form."

My brows pull together. "But you're as strong as a human with invisible tentacles."

He pauses for a moment, and my stomach tightens. I've only known him for two days, but when he's in the dark, he always hesitates to tell me what he believes to be a disconcerting truth.

"We're mates, right?" I walk around the desk and place a hand on his cool, damp tentacle.

"Of course."

"Which means I'll accept you no matter what."

"You may not when you discover what I wish to do."

"Tell me now." I give his tentacle a gentle squeeze. "There's no point in holding back when I can ask you the same question in the light of day and get a candid answer."

He blows out a weary breath. "My kind cannot survive long in other dimensions without feeding."

I nod. "You explained that to me last night."

"The only way to stay here permanently would be to absorb another human in their entirety—not just their fear."

"You mean eat them?" I ask.

"I wouldn't put it in so many words, but if I can wrap my shadow around another being and consume what makes them human, I will no longer have to keep feeding on terror."

My throat tightens. "Mr. Roberts would die?"

"I would break down his components for my own consumption, and there would be nothing left of him but skin."

Different scenarios play through my mind, and my breaths quicken. If we let Mr. Roberts go, he'll run straight to the police or some other high authority and tell them he got attacked by a talking tentacle man. And he'll point the finger at me for harboring him.

I could ask my mate to escape to his dimension, but he would refuse. And he's already absorbed too much humanity to return safely. Going on the run would be impossible with no money, and the authorities would catch up with us anyway.

But does my boss deserve to die? Under any other circumstances, I would say no, but keeping him alive will certainly cause us more trouble than we deserve.

"Mate?" he asks.

"Do it," I say.

"Are you sure?"

"It's the only way we'll be together."

"But you will come to fear and revile me."

"I won't," I say from between clenched teeth. "That bastard stole four years of my dreams, making me believe nobody wanted my art. He also spent that time profiting from my work, while keeping me here as cheap labor."

"Very well."

"Wait," I blurt. "If you absorb Mr. Roberts, will you look like yourself or like him?"

"I will take on his form while digesting him. After that, I'm free to change my shape back to one you find pleasing."

Pressing a palm to my chest, I exhale the longest breath of relief. "This might work."

"Then step away."

I take several backward steps toward the door and lean against its hard surface. My mate spreads out his arms, the way he did when he first entered my bedroom, and tentacles stretch out from his middle.

There are so many that I lose count after twelve as they twist and tangle across the room. When the appendages reach Mr. Roberts's unmoving form, I stiffen.

"Do you want to close your eyes?" my mate asks.

"No," I reply. "We're in this together, and I accept every part of you."

The tentacles form a cocoon around Mr. Roberts's body, and drag him across the floor. When they reach my mate, the bundle of appendages rises to his torso.

Every fine hair on my body stands on end as I remember that octopuses keep their mouths in the center of their tentacles.

If the tentacles came from his torso, then does it mean his mouth was always in his stomach? I try casting my mind back to all the times I noticed him eat, but it's impossible to remember what he did in the dark.

"Are you alright?" I ask.

"This prey is larger than expected," my mate replies, sounding like his belly hurts. "I will need to rest for some time to ease the digestion."

"I'll tell everyone not to disturb Mr. Roberts."

"Thank you," he murmurs, sounding sleepy.

I step out of the office, into the locker room and close the door. Ryan hovers by the cleaning cupboard and turns to me with his brows raised.

"What happened with Mr. Roberts?" he asks.

I shake my head. "He had a dizzy spell while telling me off about being late, and I helped him on the sofa. Then he asked me to turn off the light so he could have a rest."

Ryan shakes his head. "I'd like to take a power nap during the middle of the day."

I raise a shoulder and walk through the locker room and out to the shop floor.

For his sake, Ryan had better not go into that office.

Chapter Fourteen

Mr. Roberts's accomplice still sits at her table, scrolling through her computer tablet while sipping an espresso. A lock of blonde hair falls loose from her chignon and she sweeps it behind her ear with a manicured finger.

I walk past the counter, my heart pounding even harder than it did two nights ago when I first found my mate standing at the foot of my bed. If what Mr. Roberts said was true, then she either sold my paintings knowing they were stolen, or I'm on the cusp of becoming a paid artist.

In a way, that's more terrifying than a nightmare because selling my work to people who appreciate it is beyond my wildest dreams.

Jessika clears tables on my far left. As soon as our eyes meet, she jogs up to me with a frown. "Are you alright?"

"Not really." I give my head a shake.

"Come here." She pulls me to the corner, but I try to shrug her off. Then she grips my arm, forcing me to look into her eyes.

"What's wrong?" I ask.

"Shouldn't you be telling me?" She gives me a meaningful stare.

"No." My gaze darts to the woman who sets down her coffee cup, looking like she wants to leave. "It's complicated. Can it wait?"

"Not until you explain why you haven't bonded with your umbra."

I blink. "What did you say?"

"The handsome blond with the gray sweatpants?" She flashes her eyes. "That's how the unbonded ones all camouflage when exposed to the light."

My throat suddenly feels extremely dry, and I place a hand over my mouth. I've felt so off-kilter this day and a half that I haven't had time to ask her hard questions, which is crazy because I'm not usually so easily distracted.

I lean into her and whisper, "What do you know about them?"

She glances over my shoulder. "Is Mr. Roberts coming back anytime soon?"

"No." The word slips from my lips before I can even stop it. "I mean, I don't know."

"Your umbra's absorbing him, yes?"

I keep my features perfectly still because if she knows so much about where my mate originates, I don't need authorities from another dimension coming over to arrest us.

"It's alright," she says with a tiny smile. "That's what umbras do if they want to stay in our dimension for the long term."

"Right." I run my fingers through my curls. "He didn't tell me any of this."

"Neil and I needed help to work things out when he first crossed over."

"You're human, right?" I whisper.

"Yes," she says with a smirk. "Are you?"

"I'm confused that you know so much about them."

"It's only because someone else told us how things work."

Jessika tells me that the umbras are a race of shapeshifters who live in the deep waters of a world that suffers from global warming. Over the millennia, they developed a way to cross dimensions, but creating the rift requires getting a summons from a soul mate."

"So who put the meditation on Youtube?" I ask.

She raises a shoulder. "Probably another umbra who crossed over early and wants to help others. But you realize the only way for your mate to be with you properly is by absorbing another human?"

My features tighten. "I see."

"Is yours with Mr. Roberts?"

A pang of guilt strikes my chest. It's one thing to justify Mr. Robert's demise to myself. Quite another to admit it to Jessica. I have to remind myself that setting him free would have hurt an innocent monster. I give Jessika the subtlest of nods, not wanting to throw my mate under the bus, but I'm desperate for information on what happens next.

Jessika places a hand on my arm. "It should take about three hours to digest someone of Mr. Roberts's size, but make sure he uses that form when out in public."

"Why?" I ask.

Jessika stares at me as though I've been struck dumb. "So he can take over the coffee shop, of course. I'm going to need a place to work until Neil gets his first check."

My heart skips a beat, and I glance around the busy café. "You mean all this will be his?"

She grins. "It's how the umbra get settled so easily in this dimension. But you've got to make sure he takes on Roberts's appearance for at least a few weeks before starting to make subtle changes."

I give her a blank look. This is a lot to take in.

Jessika wrinkles her nose. "Do you honestly want to be seen in public with Mr. Roberts?"

"I don't mind as long as it's not him on the inside," I reply with a shrug.

She gives me a sympathetic pat on the arm. "It looks like you and your mate are all set. He should absorb all of Roberts's memories but none of his personality, and when you're in private, he can shift back into a more gorgeous form."

My breaths become shallow, and every fear about my mate and I being chased by the law evaporates with the steam rolling off the barista machines. But there's something I need to know.

Glancing around to check that no one has moved closer to our conversation, I lean into her and ask, "What do they look like in the dark?"

"They're shapeshifters," she replies with a frown. "Does it matter?"

"I'm curious."

She reaches into her apron, pulls out her phone, and scrolls through the photos app. "Here we are."

The first image she shows me is of a near identical copy of my shadow mate when I first saw him in my bedroom, except that she's adjusted the camera settings to take pictures in the dark. She turns on the brightness and makes the image more detailed.

What I first thought had been a manly outline turns out to be a mass of tentacles shaped to create muscular biceps. Now it makes sense how he could stretch his arms across the room. They were actually tentacles. And the masculine outline was him shifting into something appealing.

"So, my mate is a giant, shapeshifting octopus?" I ask.

"Not anymore." She flashes me a grin. "He'll be humanoid from now on, even in the dark."

"But the tentacles?" I give her a meaningful look.

"He'll still be able to manipulate them, but they'll be invisible unless he makes an effort to let you see them."

I nod because that sounds so familiar. "Thank you."

Jessika claps me on the shoulder. "Well, that's all I wanted to ask. I'm glad you both chose Mr. Roberts. At least your mate won't need to scramble about for a job."

She walks back to the counter, leaving me standing by the wall for several moments, reeling from all the new information. I now have a gorgeous and wealthy mate who would kill to protect me. Best of all, I'm also a real artist.

I glance around at the tables, where the woman from earlier walks back to her seat with a fresh cup of coffee.

My heart skips, and I feel myself walking toward her on wooden legs.

"E-excuse me?" I croak.

She casts me a dismissive glance before returning to her tablet.

"Mr. Roberts told me you were interested in purchasing more of my art?"

Her attention snaps back to me, and she sweeps her gaze up and down my form. "If you're talking about the watercolors, Gordon told me he paints them in his attic."

"That's me." I point in the direction of the ceiling. "I'm the one who lives up there. I'm the one who produces the paintings."

The look she gives me is cold and unimpressed. For the next several seconds, she remains silent. It's either an attempt to intimidate or to make time to think.

Finally, she says, "Then I congratulate you for being so prolific, and I look forward to selling more of your pieces."

"Where?" I ask.

Her lips purse.

Irritation grates across my skin like sandpaper. "Where do you sell my paintings?"

"The art gallery I manage," she says, sounding defensive.

Something's off about her. Most people would question my claims of being the artist, but she accepted it too quickly for my liking. I have no doubt that she knew Mr. Roberts wasn't the real painter.

"I hope you enjoy the profits you made because you won't be getting any more works from me."

Her jaw drops. Before she can say another word, I turn on my heel and walk around the counter. There's no way I ever want to associate with that snobby shrew.

For the next hour, I make cappuccinos, café au laits, and hot chocolates. My thoughts switch between cursing myself for being so rude and congratulating myself for standing up to the stuck up customer. The only way I can remain calm is by assuring myself that my art must have commercial value if Mr. Roberts stole so much of it to sell to that woman.

It's time for me to start believing in myself and to move forward with the new life I'll have with my exciting new mate.

Hours later, an imposing presence appears behind me and I turn to the doorway to find Mr. Roberts standing in his usual attire, looking at me like I'm a hot chocolate with whipped cream.

My heart flips like a panini. Which version of my mate will I get? The kind-hearted one or the wicked one?

"Uh oh," Ryan mutters from my side. "Looks like you're in trouble with the boss."

"Yeah," I reply with a nervous giggle.

"Alexis," he says, using the exact inflections as Mr. Roberts. "Follow me."

Chapter Fifteen

My heart skips several beats as I walk through the coffee shop toward my mate. I'm ninety-nine percent certain that it's him, even though he's doing a convincing job of acting like Mr. Roberts.

There's no way a skinny coward like my former boss could ever defeat a huge creature with tentacles, especially when unconscious and in the depths of his belly.

Jessika gives me a thumbs up in my periphery, and I suppress a surge of excitement, tinged with a bit of trepidation. Which version of my mate will I see when we meet in private? The gentle one, the wicked, or a completely different version who has picked up Mr. Roberts's personality traits?

A shudder runs down my spine. I hope for both our sakes that Jessika is correct about umbras only assimilating the knowledge of the person they consume.

I walk past my mate, who leans in to sniff my hair, making my scalp tingle. He has never done that before, but if he truly was a water dwelling creature who took the shape of an octopus, maybe he didn't have such an acute sense of smell?

He follows me through the back room. Instead of continuing toward the locker room and to Mr. Roberts's office, I take a left toward the security door that leads to the living quarters.

The door slams shut behind us, and a set of invisible tentacles wrap around my waist, turn me around, and pull me into a broad chest.

"Oh." I fling my arms around his neck. "It's really you."

His strong arms wrap around my back, thick ropey muscles that certainly don't belong to Mr. Roberts. I lean into his shoulder, inhaling the scent of freshly roasted coffee.

This moment is utter perfection. Not only do I have a mate of my own, but he's both a man and a creature with tentacles for quadruple the pleasure.

"Did you ever doubt me?" he says, sounding like his daytime self.

"Not really." I pull back and gaze up into his handsome face.

He doesn't look so much like his angelic self anymore. His skin is darker, with hazel eyes instead of bright blue, and hair a deep mahogany that's even richer than Mr. Roberts's.

"Is my appearance pleasing to you, my mate?" he asks.

I tilt my head to the side and smile. "You're everything I could ever have hoped for and more, but do you still need to feed on my tears?"

He pauses, the corners of his lips quirking into a smile. "I don't know, should we go upstairs and check?"

A jolt of arousal hits me straight in the clit, making my empty core pulse. Widening my eyes, I step back. "You're not going to—"

"I ate a sandwich before leaving Gordon Roberts's office," he says. "So, I don't need anything from you to survive, but I'd like to see if I'm still addicted to the taste of your pussy."

One of his invisible tentacles pulls my hips flush against his thick erection. My insides turn to warm mush.

"I also want to fuck you with a real cock," he growls.

"Now?" I whisper.

He releases me, the grin on his features wicked. "You have a head start. After a count of ten, I'll give chase and I won't even use the tentacles."

"Wait." My voice trembles, because my clit still throbs from last night's pussy whipping. "What happens if I get away?"

"Then you get to ride me like a cowgirl," he says with a broad grin as though he's drawing on one of Mr. Roberts's memories.

"And if you catch me?"

"Then I'll fuck you in all holes until you're howling my name. Countdown starts now!"

My heart jolts into action, powering my feet. I race down the hallway and up the stairs, taking the steps two at a time. The wood creaks underfoot, causing an awful ruckus, but I quicken my pace.

For the first time ever, I try the door of Mr. Roberts's apartment. It's open, and I step inside. What I see next makes my jaw drop. He's arranged it into an open-plan living room and kitchen with polished wood floorboards and designer furniture in multiple shades of gray.

Dozens of my watercolors hang on the pristine white walls, providing vibrant displays of color. My paintings are abstract, mostly reflecting dreams and snatches of my imagination, but the way he's displayed them makes my knees buckle.

"Ready or not," my mate roars. "Here I come!"

I'm still too awed by the beautiful surroundings to

register his words. There's a silver rug on the floor that looks like it's come straight from a magazine and delicate lights that hang from the ceiling like fallen stars.

How much of this luxury apartment did Mr. Roberts finance with money he made from stealing my art?

Strong arms wrap around my waist and pull me into his chest.

"Shit," I shriek, my heart jumping into my throat. "That's the shortest ever countdown."

"Got you," he growls, his appendages encasing my entire body like a cocoon.

"You said you wouldn't use your tentacles."

He presses his lips on the side of my neck, sending tiny implosions of pleasure across my skin. "I said I wouldn't use them to catch you," he murmurs into my curls. "Now that you're caught, I can do whatever I please."

I squeeze my thighs together, trying to staunch a surge of arousal at the prospect of getting fucked with my mate's hard cock.

"Do you know what to do?" I ask.

"The man whose knowledge I absorbed watched hours of pornography," my mate murmurs. "I'm surprised human women can climax from a partner with only two hands, a tongue, and a cock."

"They're probably faking it for the camera."

He huffs a laugh. "That doesn't surprise me at all."

My mate carries me through the apartment like I'm his quarry. As we pass a kitchen of white units and black marble worktops, the resentment I'm holding evaporates in the heat of his body. My days of loneliness and poverty are over. This place, along with the entire building, now belongs to my mate.

He continues up a floating staircase to the apartment's upper level, and into a luxury bedroom that looks like something out of a hotel. My breath catches, but my mate only seems interested in pressing a tentacle between my thighs.

"Do you have a name?" I ask, not knowing what to howl when we're fucking.

"Outside, I'll use Gordon Roberts, but when we're alone, I want you to call me Mate."

"Why?"

"Because I might have the body of a human but my soul belongs to you."

My heart melts as his tentacles unfasten my barista apron. The fabric drops to the floor with a gentle thud.

When he doesn't slip his tentacles beneath the rest of my clothes, I ask, "You're not tearing it off?"

"And ruin a perfectly good uniform?" he replies. "Besides, I want to watch you strip."

"R-really?"

Releasing me, he backs toward the wall and folds his arms. Old habits die hard, I suppose.

"Take it all off," he says in a voice that's so low and husky that I feel it in my pussy.

This time, when I'm unbuttoning the shirt, my fingers tremble but that's out of excitement, rather than terror. My mate's gaze burns like molten fire as I reveal my bra and then my belly. By the time I unfasten my pants and drop them to the floor, he's reaching down to adjust himself.

"Human clothing is overrated," he grumbles. "I never knew erections could be so uncomfortable."

I gaze down at the huge tent in his pants and lick my lips. "But you had one before."

"It was just my camouflaged mating arm."

That's when I remember that octopuses don't technically have penises, just a specialized tentacle. Fortunately, my mate is also now a fully-formed human.

"Come here," he growls.

"But I haven't finished undressing." I step out of my fallen pants and toe off my loafers.

One set of invisible tentacles snake around my back and unhook my bra with the dexterity of fingers, while the other slips beneath my knickers and eases them down my thighs.

My heart flutters. This is the first time he's undressed me with those appendages, and I hadn't expected him to be so smooth. Before I can ask if he's using Mr. Roberts's knowledge, his tentacles lift me off my feet.

"What are you doing?" I ask with a shriek.

"Since I caught you, I call the shots," he says, his voice a low growl. "And I want to taste your pussy with my mouth."

A jumping-off-the-diveboard sensation makes my stomach dip as I remember that this is also the creature who pulled Mr. Roberts into a maw situated in his middle. "Which mouth?"

"This one." He snaps his teeth.

My stomach muscles untighten, and I relax in the grip of his tentacles. "Oh."

He pins me to the wall, so my crotch is nearly six feet off the ground. Strong tentacles wrap around my shoulders, my thighs, my knees, both keeping my legs open while holding my body in place.

He stands between my spread thighs, his gaze fixed on my pussy. A cold draft swirls around my heated skin and settles on my clit, which is still a little sensitive from last night's whipping.

"You're so wet for me," he says in a deep voice that charges the air with electric tension.

His breath, which was once almost as cool as the breeze is now warm and gusting against my exposed sex. Every inch of my flesh shivers for his touch.

"Please," I say from between clenched teeth.

"Ask nicely and say my name."

My throat closes, and I have to force air from my lungs. "Please, Mate. I want you to lick my pussy."

He makes a satisfied rumble that goes straight to my empty core. The muscles there clench, and right now, I don't know which I want more—his tongue or his cock.

"Since you asked so prettily," he says with a broad grin and brings his mouth to my pussy.

The first lick his from a human tongue. I'm so sensitive that I feel every taste bud pass over my folds. My thighs tremble as he continues to lap, savoring my taste with appreciative moans.

"How is it?" I ask with a gasp.

"Still delicious," he mumbles into my pussy, sending vibrations of sound across my entire pelvis.

My eyes roll toward the back of my head. I want to close my thighs around his ears, but the tentacles holding them open are too strong.

I lose myself in the movements of his perfectly human tongue. His back and forth strokes over my clit are wonderful and the slurping and swallowing sounds make my skin tingle. The pleasure he gives me is gentle, slow, and nothing compared to last night or the night before.

Clutching the thick tentacle around my chest, I dig my fingers into the invisible flesh, my pussy clenching with need.

"Please," I cry out. "I need your fingers inside me or your tentacles."

Something warm and slippery circles my asshole, sending a skitter of pleasure down my spine.

"My pussy," I say with a whimper. "I'm begging you, please."

"Be a good girl and wait for my cock," he mumbles

around my clit. "I'm going to fuck you so hard, you'll be streaming tears."

My heart flips. He sounds more like his wicked self.

He clamps his lips around my sensitive bundle of nerves, just as his tentacle pushes into my ass and stretches me wide. Then my first orgasm of the day tears through me like a cyclone.

I convulse within his grip, my legs thrashing, but his tentacles hold me in steady. He pulls his head back, and gazes up at me, his eyes dancing.

"Nice, but it's not the same without watching your entire body," he growls.

"S-so that's why you liked standing at the edge of the bed," I murmur.

"Seeing you tremble under my tentacles is the biggest pleasure of all."

"Please," I say with a whimper.

"Please, what?" he replies.

"Please fuck me with your tentacle cock."

Chapter Sixteen

He draws back again and looks me in the eye. "Do you know what you're saying, Little Mate?"

"I want to see you." My throat convulses, but I continue. "If that's possible."

His eyes crinkle around the edges. "And if you're scared of what you see?"

"I already have a good idea of what you look like when you're not shapeshifting. The moonlight didn't hide everything, you know." I run my hands down his clothed chest, letting him know how much I want every bit of him.

His brows rise, and a thrill of excitement runs through me at the thought of seeing all of my mate.

"I've assimilated too much of Gordon Roberts to be able to change back to my old shape, but I can make my tentacles visible."

"Please," I say, my voice breathy.

The buttons of his shirt unfasten themselves, and invisible tentacles pull off his clothes, leaving him standing in front of me naked. My gaze roves over his muscular abs and chest, but the air around his torso ripples. Flesh colored appendages appear from his sides, seemingly coming from nowhere.

My lips part to let out a shocked gasp. "I thought they'd be black."

"They take on any color, depending on their surroundings," he replies, his voice warm. "Right now, they're the exact shade of your skin."

I run my hands over the smooth tentacles, which are only slightly damp. "Why aren't they slippery?"

"Is that what you want?"

I nod.

"My little mate is getting a tentacle fetish," he says with a chuckle.

I glance down at the appendages wrapped around my body. "Which one's your mating arm?"

"This one." A thinner tentacle rises between our bodies. While the others are thicker than my thighs, his mating arm has the girth of my forearm.

My fingers tremble as I run my hands up and down its warm surface. It's a little rougher than his regular tentacles with ribbed skin on the smoother side and tiny suckers on its underside. It tapers at the tip with a fleshy head that ends in a gentle point.

The head is about twice the thickness of my thumb. As I rub the peculiar growth, it splits into dozens of tiny tendrils.

"Oh." I snatch my hand away. "What is that?"

He strokes my arm with the threadlike projections, sending a tingle down my spine.

"All the better for stroking your cervix and exploring the parts of your little pussy that no human penis can reach."

My tongue darts out to lick my bottom lip, and he growls his approval.

"Do you want me to fuck you with my mating arm?" he asks.

Gulping, I give him a slow nod. "But you know, something as long and thick as that will never fit."

His deep growl resounds across his tentacles and makes every inch of my skin tingle. "You'll take my tentacle cock like a good little mate."

My pussy muscles clench, seeming to agree.

"Alright," I whisper, "But you'll need to give me extra lubrication."

He reaches between my legs with his human hand and slips two thick fingers in my pussy and stretches me open. "You're so wet."

I make a strangled sound in the back of my throat.

"It looks like you're doing well enough on your own," he adds.

"Just fuck me," I whisper.

With a deep groan that I feel to the marrow of my bones, he pulls out his fingers and rubs the tip of his mating arm over my pussy. The little tendrils stroke every fold, and some of them make tiny flicking motions over my swollen clit.

Pleasant tremors run across my nerves, making me throw my head back and moan.

"You like me playing with your pussy?" he asks.

"Oh." I grip the tentacles holding me against the wall. "This is just like getting whipped, only without the sting."

My mate lets out a deep purr that I feel across every inch of my skin. "I will never cause you pain unless it's what you want."

"Promise?" I ask with a giggle.

"I swear it." Some of his tendrils sweep gentle circles around my opening, and the ones toying with my clit make every muscle in my pelvis pulse.

"Your sweet ass is gripping me so well," he says in a deep

voice that fills the room. "I can't wait to feel how you'll tighten around my mating arm."

"Please," I whisper.

"Please, what, mate?" he asks, his voice laced with amusement. "You're a human. Use your words."

I huff a hysterical laugh, but my mind is too addled to come up with a clever response.

"Fuck me," I say from between clenched teeth. "Fill me with that mating arm while you're giving it to me up the ass. And while you're at it, I want another tentacle sucking my clit."

"I can do better than that."

Before I can ask what he means, he pushes his ribbed cock inside me. The stretch is so intense that it steals my breath for several moments. Pleasure explodes across every nerve ending, making them light up. My eyes widen, and my mouth falls open with a gasp.

"Too big, too big," I say through breathy moans, my fingers digging into his tentacles.

"You've had bigger," he replies with a smirk. "And in a moment, you'll take more."

The sensations are so overwhelming that my eyes flutter shut as he pushes more and more of that mating arm into my pussy. I feel a slight tingle along my walls, where he adds a little extra lubrication to ease the slide, but when he reaches my cervix, the little tendrils expand.

"What." I reel forward with his tentacles holding me in place. "What's this?"

"You like it?" he purrs. "Every part of my mating arm is savoring your sweet pussy."

As he says this, the extra tendrils caress the contours of my insides with deep strokes that make my thighs tremble. Sweat breaks out across my brow, and I'm panting hard enough to warm the entire apartment.

"Pleasure like this should be illegal," I say.

"You're so tight," he growls.

My eyelids flutter, and I let out a moan.

"The way you pulse around my mating arm makes me want to fuck you like this every day for the rest of our lives."

Somewhere through the haze of ecstasy, I can't help but wonder how long creatures like him live. My lips form the words, but one of the tendrils inside me hits a spot that makes me see stars.

"Aaah!"

"Would you like that?" he says into my ear. "A century from now, I'll be taking you this exact way."

I cry out, partly out of rapture and partly with the need to ask a question. My mate adds another tendril to my g spot and another, and soon, they're taking me from all angles. The mating arm ripples and undulates inside me, each wave of the muscular cock pushing against my pleasure centers.

"Humans. Don't. Live. That. Long." I punch out every word as he drives me toward another climax.

Pleasure closes in around me from all angles, and every limb trembles with the sense that I might implode. The tentacle up my ass and mating arm work in tandem to fuck me harder and deeper than anything he's done before.

Wet sounds fill my ears, mingling with his words. "Things will be different for you, now that we're mates."

Every part of my body feels like crackles of electricity trying to detonate a fuse. But when another pair of tentacles slither up my front to seize my nipples, a burst of sensation hits me like a struck match.

Whatever my mate says next is muffled by my scream. I pulse around his thick tentacle cock, feeling its every contour. The only thing keeping me from thrashing about are the thick appendages pinning me to the wall.

He holds me in the safety of his cocoon, whispering

filthy words of encouragement as his tentacle sucks my clit through what feels like an unending climax.

It's only when the sensations fade that something registers. "What did you say?"

His hazel eyes sparkle. "You heard that, my mate?"

"Not all of it."

"Humans can live as long as we do with regular infusions of our essence." He pulls back his mating arm, leaving only its smaller tip.

I grab his flesh. "Wait, where are you going?"

The grin he flashes me is so wicked, and reminds me so much of his crueler side that my stomach dips.

"Um... Mate?" I ask.

"Remember I said I wanted to fuck you with my human cock?"

I gulp. "Yes?"

He lowers me further down the wall, and wraps his tentacles around my thighs to arrange my legs behind his hips. That's when I realize something even more peculiar about my mate.

"Wait a minute," I say, getting serious. "You have two penises?"

"One of them is technically a mating arm."

"But—"

He enters me with his human cock in one swift motion. It's larger than any I've had before and extremely thick, filling me with a fresh burst of sensations. As he pushes himself to the hilt, its thick mushroom tip rests flush against my cervix.

"Oh," I moan through panting breaths. "That's amazing."

He hums his approval. "You feel so good around my cock. You're a perfect fit. I don't have to worry so much about hurting you when I'm using this one because it's built for human physiology."

It just occurs to me that he's losing his virginity. This is the first time he's had a functional human penis.

But he sure as hell knows what to do with it when he fucks me against the wall. Hard and fast, his hips piston with thrusts that make me see the cosmos. The tentacle in my ass becomes slippery and wet, matching the movements. But when the mating arm also slips in, my mouth opens in a silent scream.

My mate holds still for a moment, letting my muscles spasm and adjust around the two cocks. The stretch is so intense that my eyes water.

"Oh, fuck." I squeeze the appendage holding me up so hard that he growls. "I'm so close."

"I want to kiss you," he says, his hot breath fanning over my lips.

"Please."

His mouth descends on mine in a kiss that's gentle compared to how he fucks me with his human cock. For the next several minutes, our tongues caress each other, and I lose myself in him.

I've never felt so connected to another person before, yet this moment feels like something I've been awaiting my entire life. Thanks to my mate, I've realized every dream that I've ever imagined.

The kiss deepens as he explores every inch of my mouth. My pussy pulses around his two cocks, and my clit feels like it's being caressed from all angles. He's penetrating almost every hole.

I would mention it, but another orgasm creeps up on me and he swallows my pleasured cries.

"Oh, fuck," he moans. "I'm going to cum."

"Which cock?" My eyes snap open.

His body trembles, and every tentacle surrounding me quivers. The mating arm inside my pussy swells, making me pant.

"Hold tight," he says from between clenched teeth.

The fine hairs on the back of my head stand erect and my skin tightens with goosebumps. I do as he says and hold onto my mate like he's about to take flight.

His first spurt hits the walls of my pussy like a small jet, and the second is a powerful gush. I tighten my grip around my mate as he rides through a double climax.

"Fuck," he says with a low groan. "All that time I spent waiting for you to summon me was worth it just for this moment."

I thread my fingers through his silky hair. "How long?"

Cradling me in his arms, he huffs a tired laugh and places me on a luxurious bed with crisp white sheets. As he crawls beside me and arranges our bodies into spoons, he murmurs, "I've lived for centuries without companionship. But none of that matters, now that I have you."

My eyelids flutter shut, and I drift into a contented sleep.

If this is what it is to feel complete, I'll take a century of it and more.

Chapter Seventeen

Five Years Later

I walk out of the attic bathroom to find the triplets have already started painting and are making a mess of their creation.

Two paint brushes hover over Frida's head, telling me she's using her invisible tentacles, while Leo and Vincent are splattering multicolored paint across the watercolor paper.

I clear my throat. "What did I tell you about waiting?"

Three pairs of hazel eyes turn to me, feigning ignorance.

"Sorry," Frida says with a giggle, "But Vincent started painting first."

Her curls bounce, and she rocks forward with a scowl, presumably from being smacked over the head with an invisible tentacle.

"Vincent," I say.

He swings around and points a chubby finger at his brother. "Leo did it."

Vincent stumbles forward with a yelp.

"Leo." I crook my finger.

He shuffles forward, his shoulders up around his ears.

"What did I tell you about hitting people?" I ask.

My youngest child's tentacles wrap around my thigh, and he buries his face into my hip.

"I'm sorry." he murmurs.

When I give him a pat on the tentacles, he pulls them away and meets my eyes with such perfect innocence that my heart melts. Warmth fills my chest at his warm smile, but I force myself to stay strong. He can't get away with hitting his siblings because he's cute.

Placing my hands on his narrow shoulders, I turn him around to meet Vincent and Frida. "And what do you say to your brother and sister?"

"Sorry Frida, sorry Vincent!" he says.

The other two rush up to Leo and give him a hug. I have to pat at the air above them to see if they're having an invisible tentacle battle, but it looks like they're serious about making up.

We're home schooling the children at least until they're mature enough to keep their tentacles under control. It's hard to explain to four year olds that other humans don't have invisible appendages, especially when the other kids they meet on play dates are also the offspring of other umbras.

Jessika and her mate, Neil, live around the corner in a large house they bought with the royalties from his first book, and they have four little boys about the same age as our triplets.

With all the money we made from selling my paintings, we bought the store next door and expanded both the coffee shop and our living quarters.

"Is this where you're hiding?" ask a deep voice that fills the attic.

"Daddy!" Three sets of feet pound across the wooden floorboards.

My mate bends down and scoops them in his arms, while his tentacles stretch across the room to wrap around my waist. He lifts me off my feet and reels me, but unlike the first time we met, I relax into his touch.

It turns out that my mate is also adept at art, but his talents extend to cooking elaborate meals, putting together delicious recipes, both for food and beverages. His creativity is the reason why we needed to extend the coffee shop, and it's now one of the busiest establishments in town.

Over the years, my mate adjusted his Gordon Roberts camouflage to reflect minor changes. People dismissed the darker tint of his hair color as upgrading his image, and he explained away his muscular frame with regular sessions at the gym. The facial features were a little trickier, and there was a short stint where he wore a bandage over the bridge of his nose, claiming that he'd had minor surgery.

He pulls me into his bundle of squirming four year olds and places a soft kiss on my lips.

"Shouldn't you be at work?" I ask.

"I arranged for the triplets to visit Jessika and Neil's quadruplets," he murmurs. "In fact, Jessika is waiting downstairs."

"Auntie Jess," they chorus and wriggle out of his arms.

Tiny footsteps thunder out of the room and down the stairs. Jessika has been a lifesaver in more ways than one. She and her mate adore children and have plenty of space for sleepovers.

I turn to my mate and smirk. "What do you have planned for us tonight?"

He growls into my ear. "First, I'm going to fill every hole imaginable, then I'll fuck you so hard with my cocks, your screams will shatter the windows."

END

. . .

145

You're 99% sure that the boogie man is visiting your bedroom at night.

Every morning when you wake up, your clothes are shredded with sharp claws. He's even started stealing your underwear.

The only thing keeping you safe from his claws is your enchanted locket.

You've told the police, but they say it's probably just you trashing your room while sleepwalking.

So, one evening, you set up your phone to record him and then you go to sleep.

The next morning, watch the recording to find a man with black wings rushing toward you before hitting an invisible barrier. Then he flies into a rage and tears up everything he can find.

As he reaches your phone, you press pause... To find the most beautiful man scowling into the camera.

Intricate black tattoos cover his muscular body and he's clutching your underwear in his huge hands.

But none of that matters because you're too busy staring at his forked cock that glistens with faerie dust.

It's time to capture the boogie man.

Click here to read Stalked by the Boogie Man

About the Author

I write dark contemporary and paranormal romance featuring villains, monsters, morally gray heroes, and the women who make them feral.

When I'm not writing steamy scenes, you'll probably find me at my TikTok, @SiggyShadeAuthor

Join my newsletter for exclusive short stories and updates on upcoming books: www.siggyshade.com/newsletter

Also by Siggy Shade

Stalked by the Boogie Man

Swallowing Water